The
GIFTED,
the
TALENTED,
and Me

The GIFTED, the TALENTED, and Me

WILLIAM SUTCLIFFE

BLOOMSBURY

NEW YORK   LONDON   OXFORD   NEW DELHI   SYDNEY

BLOOMSBURY YA
Bloomsbury Publishing Inc., part of Bloomsbury Publishing Plc
1385 Broadway, New York, NY 10018

BLOOMSBURY and the Diana logo are trademarks of Bloomsbury Publishing Plc

First published in Great Britain in May 2019 by Bloomsbury Publishing Plc
Published in the United States of America in September 2020
by Bloomsbury YA

Bloomsbury books may be purchased for business or promotional use. For
information on bulk purchases please contact Macmillan Corporate and
Premium Sales Department at specialmarkets@macmillan.com

Library of Congress Cataloging-in-Publication Data
Names: Sutcliffe, William, author.
Title: The gifted, the talented, and me / by William Sutcliffe.
Description: Hardback. | New York : Bloomsbury Children's Books, 2020.
Summary: Fifteen-year-old Sam is happy to be ordinary, but when his family
suddenly gets rich, moves to London, and enrolls Sam in a school for the gifted
and talented, he struggles to find his way.
Identifiers: LCCN 2020020275 (print) | LCCN 2020020276 (e-book)
ISBN 978-1-5476-0420-3 (hardcover) • ISBN 978-1-5476-0652-8 (e-book)
Subjects: CYAC: Ability—Fiction. | High schools—Fiction. | Schools—Fiction. |
Moving, Household—Fiction. | Family life—England—London—Fiction. |
London (England)—Fiction. | England—Fiction.
Classification: LCC PZ7.S9666 Gif 2020 (print) | LCC PZ7.S9666 (e-book) |
DDC [Fic]—dc23
LC record available at https://lccn.loc.gov/2020020275
LC e-book record available at https://lccn.loc.gov/2020020276

Typeset by RefineCatch Limited, Bungay, Suffolk
Printed and bound in the U.S.A. by Berryville Graphics Inc., Berryville, Virginia
2 4 6 8 10 9 7 5 3 1

All papers used by Bloomsbury Publishing Plc are natural, recyclable products
made from wood grown in well-managed forests. The manufacturing processes
conform to the environmental regulations of the country of origin.

To find out more about our authors and books visit www.bloomsbury.com
and sign up for our newsletters.

For Saul, Iris, and Juno

and for any teacher who has ever given up their time
to put on a school play

The
GIFTED,
the
TALENTED,
and Me

Because we can

"COME DOWNSTAIRS, EVERYONE! FAMILY MEETING!"

Even though I was mildly curious about why Dad was back from work so early, and what a "family meeting" might involve, I stayed put in my room.

"PIZZA!" he added. "Last one down gets the Hawaiian!"

Doors slammed, footsteps thundered down the staircase, and I leaped up. After a brief tussle with Ethan in the kitchen doorway, during which Freya somehow managed to crawl between our legs and get the first slice, we all assembled around the table, eating straight from takeout boxes spread over a layer of drawings, uncompleted homework, unopened letters, and unread magazines.

Ethan, who was seventeen and hadn't worn any color except black for the past three years, announced through a mouthful of pizza, "I don't care who gets custody, but I'm not moving out of my bedroom."

"Custody?" said Mom.

"Yeah. I'm not leaving, and I'm not going anywhere on weekends."

"You've got the wrong end of the stick, love," said Mom. "We're not getting divorced."

"Oh," said Ethan. "So what's all this about a family meeting?"

Freya, who lived in a seven-year-old's fantasy universe populated exclusively by fairies, unicorns, and cats, temporarily tuned in to reality and began to cry. "You're getting divorced?"

Mom jumped out of her chair, dashed around the table, and lifted Freya into her arms. "We're not getting divorced. Don't worry."

"But Ethan said you are!"

"Ethan's wrong."

"How do I know you're telling the truth?" said Freya. "How do I know you're not just saying that to protect me?"

"Ethan!" snapped Mom. "Look what you've done. Tell Freya you made it up."

"I didn't make it up."

"You did! Nobody said anything about divorce until you piped up."

2

"I worked it out for myself."

"INCORRECTLY! WE'RE NOT GETTING A DIVORCE!"

"Why not?" said Ethan.

"What?" replied Mom. "You're asking me why we're *not* getting a divorce?"

"If you can't even think of an answer, maybe we should be worried," said Ethan.

"STOP!" said Dad. "Rewind. Stay calm. There's no divorce. I called this meeting because we have something to tell you."

"Trial separation?" said Ethan.

"No. It's good news."

This shut everyone up. The idea of good news hadn't occurred to us.

"I sold my company," said Dad, leaning back in his chair, with a grin spreading across his face.

Ethan, Freya, and I stared at him blankly.

"You have a company?" I said.

"Yes! Of course I do! What do you think I've been doing every day for the last six years?"

I shrugged.

"Well, until last week I had a company. But now I've sold it!"

He beamed at us, waiting for a response. None of us had any idea what he was talking about, or why he was making such a performance of this fantastically dull information. Freya, losing interest in the entire conversation, pulled a notebook from her pocket and began to draw.

"For a lot of money," he added.

Ethan's eyes rose from his pizza.

"When you say a lot . . . are you saying . . . ?"

"We're rich!" said Mom, leaping up with Freya still in her arms and beginning to dance around the kitchen. "We're rich! We're rich! Goodbye, Stevenage! Goodbye, cramped, boxy little house! It's going to be a whole new life! Nobody believed he could do it, but he did! He made it! We're rich!"

"How rich?" said Ethan.

"Comfortable," said Dad.

"Stinking," said Mom.

"Not stinking," said Dad. "Mildly smelly."

"Can I have a new phone?" said Ethan.

The only clue this might have been about to happen was Dad's job. Or lack of one. When Freya was still a baby, he walked out on whatever it was he was doing back then—something that involved wearing a tie and getting home after I was in bed—and installed himself in the shed at the bottom of our garden. He spent months on end squirreling around down there, dressed like he'd just

4

crawled out of a dumpster (which, in fact, he often had), and from this point on, when people asked him what he did for a living, he said he was an "entrepreneur." If he was trying to sound interesting, he sometimes said "inventor."

He was always coming and going with random bits of machinery, then occasionally he'd turn up in the kitchen wearing a suit, and we'd all be kind of, "Whoa! Who are you? How did *you* get into the house?" But after making fun of him for looking like an employable adult, none of us ever remembered to ask him where he was going.

One of those meetings must have generated a source of serious money, because at some point he stopped tinkering in the shed, upgraded his wardrobe from dumpster-diver to blind-man-stumbling-out-of-a-rummage-sale, and went off to work in a warehouse somewhere. Or maybe it was an office. I never thought of asking him. He was just my dad, going out to work like everyone else's dad. What this actually involved didn't seem important. As long as he showed up at breakfast and on weekends, and drove me where I needed to go, it didn't occur to me to wonder what he did all day.

Then there was a week when he flew off to America, carrying brand-new luggage and a floppy suit bag I'd never seen before. This time I remembered to ask what he was up to, but he just said "meetings." There was something in the way Mom wished him luck as he set off that did seem odd—the way she said it, like she genuinely meant it—but a couple of minutes later I forgot all about the whole thing.

It was just after he got home from America that our first-ever family meeting was called.

"Hang on," I said, interrupting Mom's celebration dance. "What do you mean goodbye, Stevenage?"

"You don't think we're going to stay here, do you?" said Mom. "Rich people don't live in Stevenage. They live in London! Dad's sold his company, I've handed in my notice at work, and we can finally get out of this dump and move to London!"

"But I like Stevenage," I said.

"The only people who like Stevenage are people who've never been anywhere else," said Ethan.

"I've been to the same places as you."

"No, you haven't. And you've barely read a book in your life. Your idea of culture is bowling."

"What's that got to do with liking Stevenage?"

"See? Ignorant."

I looked across at Mom for support, hoping she'd take my side, but it looked like she hadn't even heard. Her expression reminded me of the thing you see in cartoons when people's eyeballs turn into dollar signs.

"So we're moving?" I asked.

"Yes!" said Mom. "As soon as we can! To a place I've been dreaming of all my life. There are beautiful Victorian houses, and it's in London but it's near an enormous park, and even though it's expensive, it's filled with artists and musicians and publishers and creative people. It's called"—her voice dipped to a reverential whisper—"Hampstead."

"That's where we're going to live?" said Ethan.

"Yes, and there's an amazing school where the artists and musicians and publishers send their children. It's called the North London Academy for the Gifted and Talented. I've been in touch already, and we have places for all three of you. Freya, you'll be able to do as much painting as you like, taught by real artists. Ethan, you'll be able to concentrate on your music and maybe start a band. And Sam, you'll . . . um . . . you'll have a lovely time and meet lots of interesting new friends."

"I don't want new friends. I like the friends I've got," I said.

"Your friends are very nice, I know, but there's a much more exciting world out there. You're going to love it."

"Are you saying my friends are boring?"

"No! They're sweet kids."

"*Sweet kids!?* I'm fifteen, not five!"

"I'm talking about being stuck here, in Stevenage! It's this town that's boring! London's a global metropolis. The whole world is there. It's going to be fantastic!"

"You always say it's noisy and polluted."

"Do I?"

"Yes! And dirty and crowded."

"Well, we'll get used to that. Once you're a proper Londoner you hardly notice those things."

"And what is an academy for the gifted and talented, anyway? Why can't we just go to a normal school?"

"I'll show you the website. It's a holistic educational environment that fosters creativity and engagement with the performing arts."

"Sounds like a nightmare," I said.

Mom reached across the table, took my hand, and stared into my eyes. "Open your mind, Sam. Mainstream education is restrictive and conformist and obsessed with pointless targets and tests. This is an amazing opportunity to break free of all that nonsense and have your true self fostered and nourished! Even if you don't take to it right away, in time you're going to find new depths you never realized you had."

"I don't want to find new depths. I like the ones I've got already."

"Those aren't depths," said Ethan. "They're shallows."

"Wearing black, watching boring films, and playing the guitar doesn't make you deep, Ethan."

"Actually, it does," he replied.

I rolled my eyes at him, while privately wondering if he might in fact be right.

"Is this really, definitely happening?" he said to Dad, sounding more excited than I had ever heard him.

"Yes," Dad replied.

"You promise?"

"Yes!"

Ethan's face broke into an enormous grin. He leaned back in his chair, let out a long, ecstatic sigh, and said, "I can't believe it! This is like getting out of jail halfway through your sentence."

"If it's a school for the gifted and talented," I said, "shouldn't there be some kind of test to check that you actually are? Because I'm not."

"Of course you are," said Mom. "You just haven't quite hit your stride."

"We made a donation," said Dad.

"How do you know everyone else didn't make a donation?" I asked.

"Don't be so cynical," said Mom. "I've been watching for years how you kids are over-tested and crushed with stress and how uncreative the whole system is, and I've gotten you out. This is going to set you free to find out who you really are! I don't want you to just be molded into three more cogs in the capitalist machine. I want you to be unique and different and unafraid!"

"WOO-HOO!" yelled Ethan. "Go, Mom!"

"Dad's a cog in the capitalist machine," I said. "He seems to like it. So are you."

"Not anymore!" she said. "I never have to look at another spreadsheet again! That job's been eating me alive, but now I'll be free to concentrate on being there for the three of you."

"Being where?" said Ethan.

"Wherever you need me."

"Everyone's going to be so much happier," said Dad.

I was unconvinced that increased parental surveillance was necessarily such good news. Judging by the look on Ethan's face, so was he.

"And while you're at school, I'll have time to pursue my own interests," said Mom. "I'm going to buy a kiln and take up pottery!"

Nobody had an answer to this.

"It's going to be great," said Dad. "Not the pottery—the whole thing. But also the pottery. That'll be excellent. Homemade pots! Wow!"

Freya held up a drawing of a puppy, a unicorn, and a

kitten sitting on a cloud under a double rainbow. "Is this what Hampstead looks like?" she asked.

"Kind of," said Dad.

"Can I go now? Have we finished?" said Ethan, typing something into his phone as he walked out of the room.

Lost in a dream about our new life, Mom stared through the window toward where the horizon would have been if Stevenage had one.

"Dad? Do we really have to move?" I asked.

"I've worked for this all my life," he said. "Everything's going to be so much better from now on."

"But all my friends are here. Why do we have to go to London?"

"Because we can. London's an amazing city. Whatever it is you're interested in—anything from anywhere in the world—it's there."

"What I'm interested in is Stevenage."

"Why are you being so negative?"

"Why are you sending me to a school for weirdos?"

"It's not a school for weirdos. It's somewhere we think you'll all be happy. We're trying to protect you. I've made some real money for the first time in my life, and this is what money's for, more than anything else. To protect your children."

"From what? Reality?"

"I'll show you the school website. It looks amazing."

"For Freya and Ethan."

"For all of you! You're going to like it."

"You think?"

"Yes! You'll be fine. Once you get used to it."

This was deeply unconvincing.

"We're going to be so happy!" said Mom, seeming to snap out of her daydream, but the look in her eye was far, far away, as if our cramped kitchen, our thin-walled house, and the whole town we were living in had already ceased to exist.

Goodbye, Stevenage!

Mom spent the next few weeks driving to and from the dump as if gripped by an extended back-to-front version of a manic shopping spree. Going out and buying loads of stuff would have been the obvious reaction to our family windfall, but true to Mom's habit of always doing what you least expect, she chose to celebrate getting rich by throwing away everything she could get her hands on. It was like getting burgled in slow motion.

As our house gradually emptied, Ethan, Freya, and I figured out that the only way to hang on to any possessions was to hide them.

By the day the moving van came, we had hardly any furniture and had to watch TV standing up. We still had the TV only because as Mom was setting off for a thrift store I'd blocked the door and refused to move, while she gave a long speech that included lots of words like "capitalist," "brain rot," "imagination," and "creativity." I counterattacked with an even longer and more impassioned speech, making heavy use of "stealing from your own child," "video games as a vibrant art form," and "help with my anxiety about moving." It was the last one that did it. Naked emotional blackmail laced with mental-health buzzwords was always the best way to get Mom on your side.

As we drove away for the last time, following behind our strangely small moving van, Mom rolled down her window and whooped like she was on some chick-flick drive through the California desert. An old guy at the bus stop almost fell off his mobility scooter. People don't usually whoop in Stevenage.

"Goodbye forever, Stevenage!" she yelled out of the window.

"Forever?" I asked.

"YES!"

"I thought you said I could come back and see my friends."

She shot Dad a guilty look, which I spotted in the rearview mirror.

"I saw that!" I said.

"Saw what?"

"That look!"

"What look?"

"The one you gave Dad."

"I didn't do anything."

"When can I come back and see my friends?"

"Soon."

"That's what you say when you mean never."

"It means soon. After we've settled in. You'll make new friends before you know it."

"I'm too old for new friends."

"You're fifteen!"

"You don't go around trying to make new friends when you're fifteen. It's tragic."

"I'm over forty! What do you think I'm going to do? You think I don't need a social life?" said Mom.

"That's different."

"Why is it different? Listen—nobody is ever too old for new friends."

"Except maybe the Queen," said Dad.

"Your friends aren't really friends, anyway," said Ethan. "They're just people you grew up with."

"That's what friends are! As you'd know if you had any!"

"So all the best people in the world happen to live within half a mile of our cul-de-sac in Stevenage?"

"I never said they're the best people in the world! They're just my friends."

"Let's not argue," said Mom. "We're starting a new life! It's going to be fantastic!"

"I don't want a new life. I want my old life," I said.

"That's a perfectly natural reaction at your age."

"What's my age got to do with it?"

"Well, I've been reading about this, and during puberty boys often have the urge to cling on to aspects of childhood they know they're about to leave behind."

I buried my face in my hands. "Oh my God, I can't believe you just said that."

"What's puberty?" asked Freya.

"It's a change the body goes through at Sam's age."

"STOP!"

"When you become a teenager, the body changes shape and you begin to grow extra hair in new places . . ."

"STOP STOP STOP!"

"I'll explain later. I think Sam's feeling uncomfortable. Finding your parents embarrassing is part of it."

"YOU DON'T SAY!"

"Extra hair?" said Freya.

"Is anyone hungry?" said Dad. "Should we stop for a coffee? Who wants a snack? Snack, anyone? I'd love a Danish."

"They're called pubes," said Ethan.

"ETHAN!" snapped Mom and Dad.

For most of the remainder of the journey, Freya muttered "pubes pubes pubes" to herself.

Our new house was somehow both really fancy and a bit of a dump. Mom was so proud of it you'd think she'd built it herself. She led us from room to room, detailing complicated plans about how she was going to rip up the carpets and "strip the place back," even though it didn't seem like there was anything to strip back, and the only thing I liked was the carpets. I thought I heard her refer to the rotten-looking shed at the bottom of the garden as her "studio," but I couldn't be sure, because I was too busy staring out the window at the strangeness of this new place to listen to her.

Right outside, a middle-aged guy in a pair of expensive-looking ripped jeans and bright red sneakers was getting into a Mercedes, while a woman in a BMW was hovering behind his parking space with her hazards flashing, blocking the road. Behind her a man in a convertible was frantically sounding his horn and shouting insults. Across the street, a team of skinny guys in filthy clothes was carrying bucket after bucket of rubble out of the basement of an enormous house and tipping it into a dumpster.

So this was Hampstead. No puppies, unicorns, kittens, or rainbows were visible. I hadn't even walked down my new street yet, but I already sensed this was a place where rich people got very stressed about parking. Compared to the quiet little cul-de-sac of modern houses I'd come from, this felt like another universe. Back home, there were always kids playing out on the street. Here, you'd get mowed down in seconds.

Mom quickly set about filling the house with new furniture that turned out to be older than our old furniture, which had been bought new but had got old. Our new new stuff was all properly old. "Vintage" was the word she kept using, which I think must mean crappy.

Ethan took the room in the attic and painted it black. Given his choice of clothes, this worked as a form of camouflage, rendering him almost invisible.

I got the bedroom directly underneath him, which looked out over a row of tiny gardens toward the jumbled brick edifice that made up the back walls of the houses on the next block. People stacked upon people stacked upon people. Everywhere you looked.

If London really was where rich people came, the question I had was—why? Why why why?

Dad left the house every morning wearing a suit, which made me think he must have gotten some kind of job, but I never got around to asking him what it was. Everyone else spent the last month of summer vacation nesting and decorating and sanding floors and putting up curtains, but I did precisely nothing to improve the state of my room. I managed to unpack—barely—and that was about it. I didn't move any furniture, or get any shelves, or paint anything, or even put up so much as a poster. I thought if I didn't properly move in, this house where I didn't want to be wouldn't really count as my home.

Messages kept popping up on my phone from my Stevenage friends, but they were all about things I'd missed, or plans I'd never take part in, so after a while, when I realized that every time my phone pinged I felt a lonely, echoing twang in my chest, I switched off the notifications and stopped looking.

Now that I was utterly friendless, I had long, empty hours to fill, and chucking a tennis ball around my empty bedroom was the pastime I came up with. If you're bored enough, this can kill most of an afternoon relatively painlessly. It was also the only activity that allowed me to stop thinking about the clock ticking ever closer to the day when I would have to start at the North London Academy for Exactly the Kind of People I Instinctively Hated. Starting at any new school was frightening. The thought of my first day at this one filled me with bloodcurdling terror.

Only by attempting to catch a hundred in a row with

my left hand, or throw ten perfect corner-ricochets, or some other random challenge, could I stop my mind from turning endlessly back to the awful thought of the inexorable approach of the new school year.

Everyone in the family had a different way of complaining about the ball-throwing noise:

Dad—shouting.

Ethan—physical violence.

Freya—stealing the tennis ball.

Mom—telling me I seemed withdrawn and asking if I wanted to talk about my feelings.

I never took up the talk-about-my-feelings offer. Eventually, Mom resorted to trying to talk to me about why I wouldn't talk about my feelings, followed by literally begging me to make some kind of effort to be happy.

I told her I was trying, but we both knew this was a lie. I was sulking, and, quite frankly, I had every right to sulk.

When the begging failed to work, Mom told me to pull myself together and stop being self-indulgent.

I informed her there was nothing self-indulgent about being depressed when your whole life has been stolen away from you by your social-climbing parents.

She told me that kind of ludicrous and unfair exaggeration was more or less a definition of the word "self-indulgent."

I told her that was two words.

We then argued about hyphens for a while, until I stormed upstairs, slammed the door, and set about making as much noise as I could with my tennis ball.

On the last Sunday of summer vacation, over dinner, Mom announced that she'd decided to start writing a blog about creative parenting. She asked if we'd like to hear her first piece, and before anyone had time to ask what she was talking about, she cleared her throat, raised her iPad, and began to read.

"The theme is motherhood and creative rebirth," she said. "This post is called 'The Journey Begins.'"

"Can I have a barf bag?" asked Ethan.

"You don't have to listen if you don't want to."

"Okay, then my journey begins like this," he replied, walking out of the room and then heading upstairs.

Mom looked back at her screen and began to read. "*Is a life without change a life worth living? How can you nurture creativity in yourself and your children in a rushed-off-your-feet lifestyle? Is it possible in today's world to truly be yourself while also being there for your children? These are the questions I hope to answer in this blog.*

"*My family and I have just moved to London. That's hubby and me, and our three inspiring children: F___, seven and*

21

already a burgeoning artist; E___, seventeen, a highly talented musician; and S___, fifteen, a little stranded between the twin states of childhood and adolescence . . ."

"WHAT!? Is that all you can say about me? What do you mean, 'stranded'?"

"It's not a bad thing. And I haven't used your name."

"Did you call me 'hubby'? Please tell me you didn't say 'hubby.'"

"I . . . I'm not going to write this by committee!"

"Artist, musician, and . . . *stranded*. What's that supposed to mean?" I said.

"Just that you're in transition. We're all in transition. We're starting a new life."

"Who is this *for*, exactly?" asked Dad.

"Oh, that's a really encouraging thing to say. You don't think anyone's going to read it, do you?"

"No! Yes! I mean—I'm sure they will. Lots of them. I'm just interested to know who. So I can picture them."

"I haven't even finished two paragraphs and already you're all picking holes in it! Freya's the only one who's actually listened."

"Do I have to listen to anymore?" asked Freya.

"All right! That's it!" Mom slammed the iPad cover shut. "Negative negative negative. That's all I get from you guys, isn't it?"

An ashamed silence filled the room, as if everyone apart from Mom had simultaneously let out a silent but toxic fart.

"Sorry, Mommy," said Freya. "Can you read some more, please?"

Mom gestured with an open palm toward Freya, raising her eyebrows at me and Dad as if to say, "Why do you both have worse manners than a seven-year-old?"

Neither of us had an explanation.

"What I cook for you merits your attention, but not what I write, is that it?"

"No," we said.

At this point, Ethan reappeared in the kitchen. "I'm hungry," he said.

"Is that something you're telling me or your father?" asked Mom.

"Um . . ."

"We've just eaten dinner!" said Dad.

"Well, I'm hungry again."

"You know what?" said Mom. "Be hungry. It won't kill you. Or make yourself some food. I'm going upstairs to finish my blog."

"Is this your blog about how to be a good mom?" asked Ethan pointedly as the door slammed behind her.

An edgy silence fell.

"That was tactless," Dad said to Ethan.

"What did I say?"

"Why is Mommy angry?" asked Freya.

"You mustn't worry," said Dad. "She's just a bit . . ."

More silence.

"A bit what?" I asked.

"Crazy?" offered Ethan.

"She's on a creative journey," said Dad. "She's . . . I think . . . maybe she's just happy."

"I don't think it's that," I said.

"Happy people don't stomp off in a huff," said Freya. "Happy people brush their hair a lot and have picnics."

"I'm sure we'll go on a picnic soon," said Dad.

Freya looked skeptical.

"I hate picnics," said Ethan, gazing forlornly into the fridge.

"This is a big change for all of us," said Dad. "We have to be understanding with each other."

"THERE'S NOTHING TO EAT!" wailed Ethan.

Just Call Me Tony

As I walked into the North London Academy for the Gifted and Talented on the first day of school, and began the long trudge to my homeroom, my whole body felt weighed down with dread. All around me, swarms of teenagers who mostly looked like they'd stepped out of the pages of a glossy magazine greeted one another with noisy post-vacation hugs. In my last school everyone looked more like they'd stepped out of the Stevenage mall. Which they usually had.

I'm not the kind of person who knows how much things cost, but everyone seemed to glow with an aura of money and confidence, sporting fancy bags, designer clothes, the latest sneakers, complicated hairdos, and shiny iPhones. Judging by their passionate greetings, everyone looked like they'd been friends for years. And on top of that, they were all (supposedly) either gifted or talented.

Ever since hearing about this school I'd sensed that it would make me feel like a loser; what I hadn't realized was that this sensation would hit me within seconds of walking through the doors. Immediately and viscerally, I knew this was not my place and these were not my people. I just wanted to sink into the floor and disappear.

By the way I was greeted when I reached my classroom it almost seemed as if my disappearance fantasy had come true. Following a flurry of quick glances in my direction, all I saw was a wall of backs. Nobody made even the slightest attempt to acknowledge my existence, so I made my way toward the emptiest corner of the room and pretended to read a bulletin board.

After a while, a bearded man walked in, wearing brown corduroys and a white smocky shirt-type thing with a neckline low enough to reveal a hairy tuft of man-cleavage. At first I assumed he must be the teacher, but nobody stood up, or greeted him, or stopped chatting, and he didn't seem to mind, so I began to think perhaps he wasn't.

He walked over to me and said, "So you're Sam," extending a clenched hand as though he was attempting to greet me with a fist bump.

I put both hands in my pockets by way of a response.

"I'm Mr. Phillips, but just call me Tony," he said.

I nodded and tried to smile, concluding that this really was, despite all evidence to the contrary, the teacher.

"Shy?" he asked, clapping me on the shoulder.

There is nothing in this world more likely to make me feel shy than someone asking me if I feel shy, even though I don't actually think I am particularly shy, so I instinctively wanted to respond to this with something loud and shameless, just to prove I wasn't shy, but in the end I didn't, because I was too shy.

"Don't be," he said, in response to my nonanswer. "This is a friendly place. Don't think of it as a school. Think of it as a laboratory of curiosity."

"Um . . . which is my desk?" I asked, meaning, *please can we end this conversation?*

"Take your pick," he said. "We have a nonterritorial approach here. Some people find that hard to get used to."

"Um . . . I'll take this one, then."

"Do you mean 'take'? Or 'use'?"

"I . . . I don't know."

"Hey—don't look so worried. This is just the beginning. Rome wasn't built in a day."

I nodded, attempting to give the impression that I understood what he was talking about.

"So—what's your thing?" he said, perching one buttock on the corner of the desk I had just claimed.

"My thing?"

"Yeah. Art? Drama? Music? Dance?"

"Soccer," I said.

The smirk that seemed to permanently curl up one corner of his mouth froze.

"You're kidding, right?"

"No. Why would I be kidding?"

"Um . . . listen, Sam, it's perfectly natural at your age to want to challenge authority. I respect that. It can be a very healthy thing, and in a permissive environment it can be hard to find outlets for that urge. Am I right?"

"No. I just like soccer."

"Listen—if there's one word I hate using in this classroom, it's 'rules.' That's not how we operate. But your parents must have told you something about our pedagogical ethos, right?"

"Pedawhatical whatos?"

"We have a child-centered, nonhierarchical framework here. There are just a few things we insist on. Mutual respect. Inclusiveness. And no soccer."

"What?"

"Kicking is a violent act. We've found that it increases aggression and accentuates gender-stereotyped behavior. Ball games are fine, up to a point, as long as they're not competitive, but soccer is out. Soccer and smoking. Though we usually turn a blind eye to smoking."

"But . . ."

"Okay—it's attendance time. We can talk more later, Sam. Don't sweat it. Everyone loves this place eventually. It builds character."

He stood and began to clap, not to applaud his own wonderfulness (at least not entirely) but to quiet the class.

"Listen up, guys! It's attendance! Is anyone not here?"

There was no discernible response.

"Okay. Cool. Welcome back, everyone. Hope you all had a good summer. It's fantastic to see you all again. I'm sure you've all got a million stories—triumphs, disasters, break-throughs, and breakdowns—only kidding—anyway, can't wait to hear what you've all been up to—it's great to be back in the saddle again—not literally—only kidding—anyway, we'll have to catch up on news later, 'cause it's first period now, but I want you all to say hi to Sam here—he's new to our strange and amazing ways—fresh blood—only kidding—anyway, he's come here from mainstream educa-tion, so this is all completely new to him and probably kind of frightening and hard to keep up with—like a factory-farmed hen released in a forest—only kidding—anyway, I need someone to help him out and guide him through the first few days, so who's going to be Sam's buddy?"

I looked around at the class, who were all concentratedly avoiding eye contact with the teacher, as if this question had suddenly made the walls, floor, and ceiling fascinating to look at.

"No volunteer? Okay—it'll have to be you, then, Darius."

"Why me?" said a boy in skinny jeans so skinny they were basically just denim tights. His hair seemed to have been meticulously gelled in at least seven different directions, and he was wearing glasses with frames so chunky and hideous they could only be expensive and highly fashionable.

"Because of your charm and diplomacy," said Just Call Me Tony, as Darius rolled his eyes and chucked his bag on the floor, mouthing what looked like a stream of obscenities.

"Okay—that's that, then. See you all later, guys. Peace out."

Within seconds the room emptied, apart from me and Darius. I looked at him, read his T-shirt a couple of times (it said T-SHIRT SLOGANS ARE SO LAST YEAR) and thought, *Who is this freak?* He looked back at me, his eyes traveling up and down over my short, un-gelled hair, my gray hoodie and sagging jeans, and I saw on his face an expression that clearly seemed to say, *Who is this freak?*

For some reason, I got the feeling that to speak first would be conceding defeat, so I just stared at him.

He stared back.

I soon realized I was never going to win. Darius looked like the kind of kid who could go a week without speaking. Or blinking. Or eating.

"So, you're Darius?" I said reluctantly.

"Yup."

"Where do we go now?"

"Follow me."

He led me out of the room with a loping, stiff-shouldered walk that made him look like a very slow Rollerblader.

We walked down a long corridor, which was covered from floor to ceiling in artwork ranging from finger-paintings to anatomical drawings to lurid abstract scrawls and perfectly rendered still lifes. Half of it looked like it belonged in a gallery, some of it wouldn't have been out of place in an anatomy textbook, and a significant proportion could easily have been painted by a dog.

"Worst class of the week now," said Darius eventually.

"What's that?"

"Math. Nobody does anything if you cut, but I can't be bothered."

"Oh. Okay. That's good to know."

Darius stopped walking and stared at me through his hideous glasses. "Let me guess," he said. "You probably like math, don't you?"

"No," I lied. "It's so boring."

"Hm."

He turned away and kept on walking down the corridor. I followed, a few steps behind, and we went the rest of the way in silence, with me wishing I was back at my old school, and him, presumably, wishing he was at a photo shoot for an indie band specializing in suicidally depressing music.

Confidence is just shyness doing a handstand

The math class, in the end, was relatively normal, with a not particularly weird teacher-type person at the front demonstrating not particularly weird math-type stuff to a class with an only slightly above average level of day-dreaming, listlessness, bickering, and napping. It was almost enough to make me think the place might resemble an ordinary school.

This was a mistake. The second class of the morning was dance.

The teacher was Mrs. Florizel, who had a long gray ponytail and was the only person older than five who I'd ever seen wear yellow leggings.

The class started with everyone standing in a circle, holding hands, breathing with our eyes shut, "seeking to balance ourselves around the heart-center."

In any normal school there would have been an instant mutiny, but Darius and the others all complied. I was the only person who didn't.

"Close your eyes, Sam," said Mrs. Florizel, when she saw me staring aghast at my classmates, wondering if I'd found myself in a place that was more of a cult than a school. "There's nothing to be afraid of. Just let yourself go."

"Go" is exactly what I wanted to do, but I stayed put and shut my mouth and eyes.

"Bring your awareness into your body, everyone," she added.

I took a quick peek to try to figure out what this involved, but everyone was just standing motionless with their eyes closed. In the decade since starting school I must have spent hours of my life listening to teachers beg, scream, yell, and plead with kids to shut up and behave, but I had never once seen a class so still and quiet. It was like black magic.

For a moment, I wondered if I was going to be brainwashed. Or perhaps this was it, happening right now.

The brainwashing/black magic/balance exercise was followed by an hour "devising" an "urban dance" on the topic of "conflict resolution." Nobody told me what this meant, so I hovered in the background and watched, gradually figuring out that "devise," in this context, seemed to be a word that combined the meanings of "show off" and "boss each other around."

The class ended with a performance that featured Darius and a group of friends doing a writhing-around-on-the-floor breakdance, followed by the arrival of another intricately hair-gelled boy with his "crew" performing a stamping-around-pointing-at-your-own-crotch-a-lot routine. There was then a kind of stylized fighting stand-off between the two groups, which ended up with a new dance style emerging that amalgamated the two techniques and ended in a group hug.

I was put in the stamping/crotch-pointing group, but I stood at the back and did as little as possible, especially when it came to the hugging.

As I was walking (or rather sprinting) out at the end of the class, Mrs. Florizel stopped me and told me I had tried really hard. This assessment was, as it happens, a hundred percent inaccurate, but I thanked her and bolted.

You'd think this was as bad as a school day could get, but worse was to come. The low point was the English class after lunch with Just Call Me Tony. He set us the task of writing a poem describing the sensation of being born, which was apparently an exercise in "self-empathy."

I copied out the title "Being Born," then sat there staring at a blank page for ten minutes without a single poetic word coming into my head. Eventually, Just Call Me Tony appeared at my side, put a hand on my shoulder, and breathed into my ear, "Open yourself up."

In order to get rid of him, I nodded as if this insight had inspired me, and wrote down the first words that came into my head:

"Push!" said the doctor.
"Ow! It's really sore!" shouted Mom.
"Waaa waaa waaa!" I cried as I slithered out all purple
and icky
Like a massive angry tadpole.

I was beginning to think I might be getting somewhere when Just Call Me Tony told us to put our pens down and invited volunteers to "share." One by one, everyone in the class stood and read graphic accounts of being expelled from their mothers' wombs. The level of biological detail was, on occasion, truly eye-watering.

A boy called Jung-Keun, wearing pants so baggy he had to hold them up by hand, performed a rap accompanied by a beatboxing white girl swathed in a fluffy, obviously homemade garment that looked as if it might recently have been a bath mat. I may have misheard, but the rap seemed to be titled "Placenta Inventa," which didn't make a lot of sense to me, but Just Call Me Tony said it was "dope." He then turned to me and said that he could see I'd struggled to get my thoughts on paper, but he didn't want to leave me out, so how about if I "free-styled" something, inspired by what I had heard from my classmates.

"I'm not very good at freestyling," I said.

"Give it a try. Remember—confidence is just shyness doing a handstand. Yeah?"

"I can't."

"There's no right or wrong."

"I really can't."

"Maybe you could freestyle something about how you're feeling right now. That can help overcome social inhibitions."

"I don't think it would."

"Give it a try. Marina, would you beatbox for him?"

Marina, the bath-mat girl, threw me what looked like an apologetic glance and began to beatbox.

Everyone was watching me. I had to say or do something, but I couldn't think what.

I stood there with the eyes of the whole class drilling into me, feeling my mouth go dry and sensing my status sink with every passing second from irrelevant nonentity to whatever is below that.

After a while—perhaps an eon or two—Marina stopped beatboxing. Silence filled the room, with everyone still staring at me expectantly.

"Keep going, Marina," said Just Call Me Tony. "Let's roll with this."

Marina shook her head.

"What's up?" said Just Call Me Tony.

"If he doesn't want to do it, he doesn't want to do it."

"Okay, that's coming from a good place. I feel you, Marina, but I want to take this a little further."

Just Call Me Tony began to drum on his thighs, wrinkling his nose and biting down on his bottom lip as if he had hit on a particularly deep groove.

"Go for it, Sam," said Just Call Me Tony. "Tell us what you're feeling."

"Um . . ."

"Don't be self-conscious," he said. "Nobody's judging you."

I looked out at the class, a sea of eyes all radiating intense waves of either scorn or pity.

"I'm feeling . . . a bit weird," I said eventually. "I don't know what to say."

"*I'm feeling kinda weird 'cause I dunno what to say!*" replied Just Call me Tony, in time to his drumming. "*I'm feeling kinda weird 'cause I dunno what to say! I'm feeling kinda weird 'cause I dunno what to say!*"

After a while—an excruciatingly long while—Just Call Me Tony brought his "freestyle" to an end and said, "Okay, guys. So we've seen something interesting here about how uncertainty is a valid emotion, and how rhythm can be as important as word choice for communicating a poetic concept. I think I'll bring in some Wordsworth and some Run DMC so we can work on that further tomorrow. Cool work, Sam. You're loosening up already. That's a great start."

The longest speech Ethan had made since he was twelve

"So how was your day, everyone?" Mom asked, as we sat down to dinner at the end of what had felt like the most grueling and humiliating day of my life.

"What is *this*?" replied Ethan, with an expression somewhere between revulsion and disbelief. "*Salad?!*"

"Yes," said Mom. "Pomegranate and feta tabbouleh with sun-dried tomato, watercress, and lamb's lettuce. Say cheese, everyone. I'm going to take a quick snap for my blog. Try not to look so miserable."

"I'm going to make a sandwich," said Ethan.

"Oh, can't you at least try it?"

"Not gonna happen," replied Ethan, wandering toward our new fridge, which was roughly the same size as our old kitchen.

"Don't talk to your mother like that!" said Dad. "She's cooked you a meal!"

"Cooked?"

"Well . . . assembled."

"It's really healthy!" said Mom.

"If he's having a sandwich, I'm having one too," I said, following Ethan to the fridge.

"Just taste it! It's really nice," said Dad, taking a large mouthful. We watched him chew, gauging the (obviously quite enormous) effort he was putting into maintaining an enthusiastic facial expression as he forced his food toward the back of his mouth, then, eventually, down his throat.

"Delicious," he said, taking a large swig of water. "What are you staring at? Come back to the table. Both of you."

"Shhh," said Mom, putting a hand on his forearm.

"Why are you shushing me? Are you just going to let them wander off in the middle of a meal?"

"We have to encourage and discuss, rather than threaten and discipline," said Mom.

"What?" said Dad. "Since when?"

"In that case, I'm having ice cream," I said, opening the freezer.

"Put that back!" Dad barked.

"Encourage and discuss," said Ethan, in his high-pitched Mom voice.

"Close the freezer! Right now!"

"We have to be the sun, not the wind," said Mom. "I've found a wonderful book about this whole approach. You can read it after me."

"Mm," said Dad, meaning, *No thanks, I'd rather read a washing machine manual.*

By the time I got back to the table with my sandwich, Freya was midway through a rapturous account of her first day at the new school. It was immediately clear that she loved it almost as much as I hated it.

". . . and the art room has *everything*, and we were in there all morning and Miss Jackson said my painting of a flying horse showed immense flair and she said we're going to do printing and sculpture and landscape work and she was wearing earrings with bees on them, which are just the best things I've ever seen."

"Wonderful!" said Mom.

"All morning?" asked Dad.

"Yeah, it was awesome."

"Were there any . . . proper classes?" he said.

"Oh, we did some other stuff in the afternoon. Maybe . . . French or something? And there was some addition for a bit but that was just sooo boring I didn't really listen."

"You can't just stop listening in the classes you think are boring," said Dad.

"Oh, it's okay—I've got a face I pull so it looks like I'm listening even when I'm not. The teacher didn't notice."

"Even if the teacher doesn't notice, you can't just pretend to listen. You have to actually do it . . . Freya?"

"What?"

"Did you hear what I just said?"

"No."

"I said you can't just *pretend* to listen."

"Why not?"

"Because you won't learn anything."

"But if it's boring I'm not going to learn it anyway."

"Not if you don't listen."

"Exactly!" said Freya, as if she'd just proved Dad wrong. Which maybe she had, because he shook his head and gave up on the conversation.

"What about you two? How did you find it?" he said, turning to Ethan and me. "You didn't spend the whole morning doing art, did you?"

"No, it was all right," said Ethan, which was possibly the highest praise I'd heard him give anything for several years.

"You like it?" said Mom, looking surprised and delighted by this Ethan-equivalent of a five-star review.

"Yeah, my teacher's pretty cool and we had this extended music class where we did some jamming. They've actually got a Stratocaster in the music room with a huge amp, so

I just held back and didn't tell anyone I played, then after a while I stepped in and, you know, when I took a solo everyone freaked."

"What, ran away?" I asked.

"No, you dork. There's a few guitarists in the class already but I reckon I'm the best, and there's this girl who has the most incredible voice—kind of a bit nu-folk, a bit indie— and a few of us talked about starting a band. There's also a girl drummer who everyone says is amazing, and another guy who's into sampling, so we're going to meet up and give it a go. See how it feels. Maybe start with some covers, then see if we can find a sound of our own. You know."

This was the longest speech Ethan had made since he was twelve. Half a decade ago. All four of us gazed at him, struck dumb, as if he had gotten up and performed a tap dance.

"Why are you staring at me?" he said after a while.

"No reason. Wow! That's great!" said Dad.

"Wonderful!" said Mom.

Ethan gave a minuscule nod and wandered off to make sandwich number two. I immediately sped up my chewing, because even though there was half a loaf left, I knew Ethan was capable of inhaling the whole thing in less time than it takes an average person to eat an M&M. I didn't get a chance to immediately stake a claim for the remaining slices, though, because before I could stand up Mom demanded an account of my day.

I didn't know what to say. She seemed desperate for good news, so I just shrugged.

"But what did you think?" she insisted. "Do you like it? Did you make any friends?"

I shoved in a last mouthful of bread and, as I chewed, ran through a number of possible responses, ranging from "It was okay" to a more honest answer along the lines of "Don't make me go back! That place is a living hell! Save me! Please!"

In the end I just said, "I'm going to make another sandwich."

With Ethan and Freya so positive and enthusiastic, I felt like I couldn't tell the truth about how I'd hated the school from the first second I walked through the doors, and how with every passing class I'd felt more and more miserable.

Mom might have guessed what I was concealing, because next thing I knew, she'd served me an immense portion of ice cream.

Sometimes it seemed like my parents never had any idea what I was thinking. Other times it felt impossible to hide anything from them. Strangely, both things were equally annoying.

"It takes a while to find your feet in a new place," said Dad. "I remember, when I was your age . . ."

This was the point at which I drifted off. There's something about the words "when I was your age" that just flicks an off switch in my ears. I heard nothing. By the time he'd finished talking, everyone else had left the room, and I managed to make my escape shortly after that.

It's just one day. Things might get better, I told myself as I climbed the stairs to my bedroom.

It's not just one day though, is it? I replied to myself, toppling like a felled tree onto the bed. *It's a whole new life. In a madhouse that thinks it's a school. And there's no escape. I'm stuck. Doomed. From now until I leave school, which is three years, in other words basically forever.*

Illicit activity behind the bike racks

I wish I could tell you that over the next few weeks I got used to my liberating new environment and made lots of fascinating new friends and came out of my shell and blossomed as I discovered hidden depths of creativity in my personality. But I can't, because that isn't what happened.

I did not get used to the school.

I did not make fascinating new friends.

If I did have hidden creative depths they remained hidden.

I got to know the other students a little better though, and realized pretty quickly that, like in all schools, the classroom was divided into cliques, but none of these cliques bore any resemblance to anything I recognized from Stevenage.

The noisiest, most dominant group was the drama clique. They had an unnerving habit of simultaneously bursting into song without any warning, and then ignoring everyone else in the class while also seeming to make sure that they had an audience.

All the girls in the drama clique were good-looking, immaculately dressed, and transmitted powerful I'm-beautiful-and-I-know-it vibes, but the ringleader was a girl named Jennifer, who was so stunning she didn't even need to try. The others all had long, blond hair and looked like younger versions of the women you see in clothes ads; Jennifer had a wild mop of pitch-black hair, bright red lips, and huge intense eyes the color of fresh coffee. It was almost impossible to be in the same room as Jennifer and not look at her. Even when you made yourself look away her presence felt like a bleeping dot on a radar screen.

While all the other drama girls seemed acutely aware of whether or not they were being watched, Jennifer was different. She had an air of such aloof confidence it was almost as if she was looking down at the world from a movie screen, even when she was in a crowded classroom. Unless I reminded myself not to, I often found myself gazing blankly at her. A few times she looked up and we made eye contact, which felt almost as embarrassing as being caught rooting around with an index finger up a nostril, but her eyes always passed on so smoothly and serenely that I never knew if she'd even noticed I was staring at her. I was that invisible.

Top guy in the drama group was Felipe, who had a strange, carefully trimmed facial decoration on his upper lip that wasn't exactly a mustache, but wasn't quite not a mustache either. A similarly indefinable almost-goatee tuft sprouted from his deeply cleft chin. At least once a week he wore leather pants. On a few occasions he was seen in white jeans, with a cashmere sweater tossed casually over his shoulders. Cowboy boots were a regular feature. His mother was reputed to be a once-famous tango star from Argentina, and his dad was a banker who wore a cravat and looked like a middle-aged Prince Philip.

Clearly, the drama crew was not for me. Equally inaccessible was the music clique. The "musos," as they always called themselves, were a reclusive but quietly self-assured group who spoke to each other in an impenetrable private language and never *ever* took off their headphones. Being a muso was more a question of attitude, fashion, and what you listened to than of having any ability as a musician.

Darius seemed to be Top Muso, and was often referred to in hushed tones as something of a genius, though his musical genius seemingly had nothing to do with anything as straightforward as playing an instrument. His dad was said to be a founding member of Bouffant Pompadour, who had supposedly pioneered French electro-pop (whatever that was) before it became big (whenever that was). As such, he was "connected." There were more wannabe bands in the school than I could count, and some of them were "managed" (whatever that meant) by Darius. Just getting him to listen to one of your rehearsals was apparently a Big Thing.

The only instrument I'd ever played was the recorder, and even though half the things I'd always thought of as uncool seemed to be considered cool in an ironic way at the North London Academy for the Gifted and Talented (shirts buttoned up to the top, cardigans, girls' hair in pigtails), the recorder was definitely not in this half. There was no way to be ironically cool on the recorder. I was always useless at it anyway.

Besides, wearing any color other than black or sporting pants that could be put on without the use of a shoehorn ruled you out from entry to the muso set. My loose-fitting blue Gap jeans were the equivalent of wearing a T-shirt saying "I'm a Young Conservative Golf-Playing Foxhunter." Though, in fact, a T-shirt with that slogan would probably seem ironic, and therefore cool.

My fashion sense (or lack of it) was even more of an obstacle with the art set, who mostly seemed to make their own clothes. Though the word "clothes" isn't quite right to describe the garments of this particular clique. The key erogenous zones were always concealed in some way or other, but they could just as easily be covered by a cut-up lampshade, a repurposed license plate, or an upcycled curtain as anything you might think of as a fabric. Most of them had hairstyles that looked like they'd thrown themselves under a lawnmower then dunked their heads in a vat of cupcake icing.

These people were never going to be my friends. None of them.

This left only a few floaters. There was Prem, the Thai chess genius, but I rapidly discovered that he didn't do conversation. There was Rex, who spent every spare second (and most class time) working on his graphic novel set on a distant space station in which (judging by the scanty outfits worn by the female astronauts) the central heating had a serious malfunction. Rex was happy to talk, but I couldn't understand a word he said, and he never made eye contact or asked me anything, so after a while I realized he was just composing dialogue out loud, rather than actually talking to me. Which isn't really a viable basis for a friendship.

Then there was Steve, who never said a word, chain-smoked on his own in the corner of the playground every breaktime, always wore a large and mysterious bunch of keys attached to his belt by a metal chain, and was reputed to carry a switchblade. Like everyone else, I kept my distance from Steve.

The only person who ever greeted me or seemed to actually notice my existence was Marina, the girl who'd been wearing a reconfigured bath mat on my first day (which turned out to be one of her more conventional outfits). Even for the fashion set, she dressed like a wild card. If she hadn't been a girl, and didn't look like she was perpetually on her way to a costume party, I might have made some attempt to befriend her, but it somehow felt safer to keep my distance and avoid eye contact.

The old me might have been confident that my classmates were all weirdos and I was normal, but as time went on my sense of what constituted normal behavior seemed to dissolve, and I began to wonder if the problem might be with me. If I was somehow cooler, or more interesting and creative, I probably would have fit right in. I might even have loved the place, like Ethan and Freya. But I've never known how to be cool, and being surrounded by people who are, and know it, just makes me shrink deeper into my shell of ordinariness.

I tried to reassure myself with the thought that there's nothing wrong with being ordinary, but I couldn't pretend there was anything good about being unpopular.

After a while, I began to think I'd have to resign myself to indefinite total friendlessness, but toward the end of my third week, at the tail end of lunch break, I stumbled across a boy who appeared reasonably normal. In the Alice in Wonderland world of the North London Academy for the Gifted and Talented, this made him a fellow freak.

People who are dying of thirst in the desert sometimes see a mirage of an oasis they think will save their life, and at first I didn't believe he could be real, but on closer examination he genuinely did seem like an ordinary jeans-and-scuffed-sneakers teenage boy.

I found him behind the bike racks. I know that sounds creepy, but when you're at a school where you have no friends—and this is not something that had ever happened to me before—the hardest thing is lunch. When you're friendless, you feel like you're wearing a bright yellow high-visibility jacket with the word "LOSER" on the back. You feel as if everyone is staring at you, noticing you standing there on your own, bored and lonely. Being alone feels like a badge of shame.

The only way to get through lunch without feeling like this badge has become a huge flashing beacon, drawing the attention of every kid in the school, is to keep walking. Standing around alone, you look like you obviously have no friends. If you're walking it's less obvious, because if you look purposeful enough you can make it seem as though you're walking from one set of friends to another.

You look busy. You look normal. Until you stop, and then you look like what you are: an outcast.

So this is what I did, every lunch period. I walked around the school, trying to disguise the fact that I was ambling aimlessly by using a hurried I'm-late-for-the-person-who's-waiting-for-me stride. In this way, I both hid my friendlessness and explored every inch of the school grounds. Around and around. Over and over.

The places where teenagers normally hide in order to break school rules were always empty, because there were hardly any rules to break. The only time I ever saw anyone in the most secluded corner of the school, behind the bike racks, was when I met Jake.

"Shit! What are you doing here?" was how he greeted me, flinching in surprise after turning his head and realizing he wasn't alone.

"Um . . . I was looking for someone," I said.

"Who?"

"They aren't here, so . . . they must be somewhere else."

"Right." He didn't seem to believe me. Unsurprisingly.

"What are *you* doing here?" I asked, hoping to divert attention from my obvious lie.

"Nothing," he said.

I looked him in the eye, and for a short while he held my gaze. Somehow, we immediately saw through one another.

He knew I was hiding and I knew he was hiding. I sensed that he was lost and lonely, and he saw the same thing in me. This all flashed between us in a wordless instant.

I momentarily felt like flinging myself into his arms, but instead I gave a tentative smile, pointed at the ball next to his right heel and said, "Is that a soccer ball?"

This was a pretty stupid question because it obviously was a soccer ball, but one of us needed to say something and this was all I could think of. Also, I wasn't really asking him to identify the inflated spherical object at his feet. What I was actually saying was, "Hallelujah! That's a soccer ball!"

A few years ago, soccer had felt like the most important thing in the universe. If I'd been sent to a non-soccer school when I was twelve, I probably would have had a breakdown. By the time I left Stevenage, it had been demoted to a mere sport rather than an actual way of life, but this first sighting of a genuine soccer ball on the grounds of the North London Academy for the Gifted and Talented felt like a glimpse of a sacred talisman.

He gave me a long stare, then nodded cautiously.

I reached out a toe and flicked the ball in the air, juggling it from left to right, then up onto a knee, where I bounced it a couple of times before letting it fall back to the ground and trapping it with my instep.

The boy stretched out a leg, rolled the ball toward him,

kicked it into the air, headed it twice, then side-footed it to me. I chested it down . . . Okay, maybe that's enough detail here . . . the point is, suddenly I knew I wasn't alone here. I was still in this crazy place, without any chance of escape, but at least there was another inmate with a spark of sanity behind the eyeballs.

"What's your name?" he asked.

I told him, and he told me he was Jake, in the year below mine. Hidden away from the rest of the school, we began a furtive kickabout.

Oh heaven! Oh joy, oh rapture!

A friend! Soccer! Soccer with a friend! A castaway spotting land wouldn't have felt any happier.

After the bell went for the end of lunch, I said, casually, "Maybe see you tomorrow," when what I actually meant was "COME BACK! COME BACK HERE! EVERY DAY! FOREVER! I NEED YOU! YOU'RE MY LAST HOPE! PLEEEEEEEEEEEEEEASE COME BACK!" Sometimes you have to tone down what you're really thinking before you let it out of your mouth.

"Okay," he said, hiding his ball under a bush. I couldn't be sure, but it sounded like there was a waver of suppressed emotion in his voice.

"See you around," he added, with a cagey smile, before turning and wandering back toward the school buildings.

Straightforward!?

After that, things improved slightly at school as I advanced from having about as much social life as a cactus to occasionally being able to communicate in brief bursts with another human being, hidden behind a heap of bikes. Yes, I really was well on my way to the lifestyle of a celebrity socialite.

Meanwhile, at home, Mom was busy with her own transformation. The garden shed had been renamed "the studio," painted duck-egg blue, and kitted out with a potter's wheel, a kiln, floor-to-ceiling shelves, and a "contemplation space." (Are ducks' eggs really blue? I have my doubts.)

Mom seemed to spend most of the day down there, then appeared in the house around the time we returned home from school with bits of clay stuck in her hair and a strange look in her eye, as if we were tiny, faraway people whose language she could barely understand.

Our old house was so small we could hardly get away from one another. Our new house wasn't actually much bigger, but because it was narrow and tall, with every room on a different floor, it was sometimes difficult to find anyone to talk to. Which made me prefer the old one. Given the choice between being constantly irritated by your siblings and not even knowing where they were, irritation, I realized, was preferable.

From time to time I sat alone in my room, reminiscing about all the squabbles, fights, and arguments we used to have in our minuscule Stevenage living room.

Ah, the good old days.

One evening, looking for Mom, I came across her laptop in an otherwise empty bedroom. The screen was blank, but it was open and the standby light was flashing. Out of idle curiosity, I pressed the space bar. The computer came to life and up flashed a draft of Mom's blog. I had nothing else to do, so I began to read.

The Germinating Seed

My journey of self-discovery is underway. The studio is fully operational at last, and after four decades of creative drought, of subjugation to the needs of others and to the

expectations of society, I have *A ROOM OF MY OWN!*
What bliss!

As soon as my first delivery of potter's clay arrived, I began
to throw. What a delicious word for it, with such a wonderful
subtext of force and play. You don't make a pot—you throw a
pot. I love that.

I won't say more about what I have made (or, rather,
thrown). I'm still finding my feet (or, rather, my hands!) so
as yet these are mere artless forms, but to have found a way
to express myself at last, not as a daughter or wife or mother,
but simply as myself, is like digging up a precious long-lost
treasure.

I am there for my children as never before. So much of my
inner self was taken over by wage-slavery that even when I
wasn't using childcare, my head was elsewhere. Now, as soon
as they arrive home from school, I can step from my studio to
engage with their hopes, fears, anxieties, and dreams.

F___ is simply soaring. Her artistic talents are at last
being recognized and nurtured. Pulling her from mainstream
education has been like releasing her from a straitjacket.
E___, too, in his adolescent way, is blossoming. He has found
a small group of like-minded musical adventurers. I am
confident that together they will forge a path into hitherto
undiscovered corners of the musical landscape. The young
are so unselfconscious and free in their patterns of thought.

For S___, things are not so easy. He's a very straight-forward boy, and the unstructured approach is a great challenge to his rigid male brain. I feel confident he'll loosen up in time, and somehow make contact with his deeply buried creative self, but for him this may not be an easy journey.

[More stuff?
Encouraging hubby? Make something up?
Something on pots as ancient symbol of fertility.
Autumn/the moon/mindfulness/seasonal eating, etc.??]

Hearing footsteps on the stairs, I hurriedly slammed down the laptop screen and sprinted for my room, then sat on my bed, one word pounding furiously around and around my head: "straightforward."

I'd never before thought of this word as an insult, but now I couldn't see it any other way. Is that really all I was? Straightforward!?

It wasn't long before Mom called us down for dinner, and as I walked to the kitchen I felt equally certain that I couldn't admit I'd read Mom's blog and that I couldn't hold in what she'd written about me.

Dinner was when the whole family got together and talked. To each other. Whether you wanted to or not. Phones were banned, even for Dad, which always made him jittery. Dad feels about his phone the way deep-sea divers feel about their oxygen tanks.

Mom never failed to ask for an account of our day, and Freya always responded first. In fact, she was usually the only one who answered at all.

While I contemplated whether to raise the issue of Straightforwardgate, Freya came out with one of her epic anecdotes along the lines of, "So-and-so said this-and-that to Such-and-such, so So-and-so-2 told So-and-so-3 that So-and-so-1 had said this-and-that which made So-and-so-3 cry until So-and-so-4 came along with So-and-so-5 and said to So-and-so-1 . . ."

I tuned out after that. Everyone did. But just watching Freya speak, taking in the movements of her face and arms, it was clear that, unlike me, she loved school and the school loved her. Every day, party invitations cascaded out of her backpack and playdate requests pinged through on Mom's phone like artillery barrages.

Dad listened to Freya's anecdote wearing the expression of someone paying polite attention to an important speech in Japanese. Ethan just ate, with the distant look in his eyes of someone listening to music on headphones (which wasn't allowed, but might as well have been for all the difference it made to Ethan's awareness of what was happening around him at the table).

When Mom turned to me for a description of my day, I opened my mouth to say, "It was fine," which was the wildly false description I gave of more or less every school day, but something strange happened. The words that came out were "I saw your blog."

Mom's listening-politely-to-Freya smile froze. Her mouth opened and closed.

"I was looking for you upstairs and your laptop was there by the bed, and it was on the screen," I said. "I didn't mean to read it, but then I kind of did."

"You read it?" said Mom.

"I couldn't help it. It was right there."

"My laptop is private."

"I thought it was a blog. Anyone can read it."

"Yes, but . . ."

"Except me. You're writing about us, and anyone is allowed to read it *except* us?"

"That's just a rough draft. It's a work in progress. You shouldn't have looked at it without asking."

"Really? Is that not *straightforward* enough for you?"

"I . . . um . . . there's nothing wrong with being straightforward. It's a great quality."

"And having a rigid male brain? Is that a quality too?"

"Rigid is another word for strong. It's an important attribute."

"If you're a roof beam."

"There's nothing wrong with it. We are who we are. And that's a private document. You shouldn't go snooping through my laptop."

"Does it say anything about me? Can I read it?" asked Ethan.

"Not yet!" snapped Mom. "They're just notes. I'm not even close to posting it."

"You're blossoming and you're a musical adventurer," I said.

"Cool," said Ethan. "Thanks, Mom. Can you put in the name of my band? Tangerine Snowflake Pissbucket."

Freya, for some reason, seemed to think this was the funniest thing she had ever heard, which probably wasn't what Ethan had intended. "Tangerine Snowflake Pissbucket!" she crowed, swaying in her chair so wildly she almost fell off.

"I don't want to hear that word again," said Dad.

"Tangerine?" said Freya.

"Don't be silly."

"Or pissbucket?"

"Stop it!"

"*He* said it!"

"He's seventeen. And he shouldn't have said it at the dinner table."

"What is a mm-bucket?" asked Freya.

"It's not even a real word," said Dad.

"And you have to have a *thing* if you want to stand a chance," continued Ethan, "so we're a queer band."

"A what?" I asked.

"A queer band," said Ethan. "Everyone in the band identifies as queer."

A confused silence fell over the table.

"Including you?" asked Dad.

"Yeah."

"Is this your way of telling us you're gay?"

"Yeah. I came out yesterday. At school. It was a very positive experience."

"You came out of what?" asked Freya. "A pissbucket?"

"Actually, I think I've always been bi-curious," said Ethan.

"I'm curious!" chirped Freya, sensing she was missing out on something. "Everyone says so!"

"I don't think you're bi-curious," said Ethan. "At least not yet."

"I am! I'm just as curious as you are!"

"Ethan!" said Mom, as if hailing him across a busy road. "Ethan, Ethan, Ethan!"

Everyone turned to look at her. There was a moment of tension as we all noticed that her eyes were glistening with tears. "This," she said, after a resonant pause, "is such *wonderful* news! I always knew there was something special about you. Something sensitive. I'm just so relieved this new environment has allowed you to get in touch with your true self, and to find who you really want to be without shame or stigma. I'm so happy for you, Ethan! You have such a rich life ahead of you, with so many adventures!"

Mom launched herself from her chair and enveloped Ethan in an enormous hug. For the past few years Ethan had been about as touchy-feely as an electric fence, but for once he actually let Mom hold him.

"Do you have a boyfriend?" asked Dad.

"That's private," said Ethan.

"Don't pry! Give him some space," said Mom. "You can be so tactless."

"Sorry," said Dad.

A few seconds later, Mom said, "Do you, though? Can I meet him?"

"I'm single! Okay?"

"Were you gay in Stevenage, or has it just happened since we moved here?" I asked.

"Oh, Sam. You're such an idiot!" barked Ethan, before storming out of the room.

Mom shot me an angry look. "Now look what you've done!" she snapped. "Honestly, the pair of you!"

"What did *I* do?" said Dad.

Mom rolled her eyes and stamped off up the stairs after Ethan.

"Well!" said Dad. "Well, well."

I looked at Dad.

Dad looked at Freya.

Freya opened her notebook and drew a unicorn.

"Ice cream?" said Dad eventually.

How I got a girlfriend for thirty seconds

But that's enough about Ethan. He's only my brother, and let's not get carried away with how interesting or important brothers are. The person I really need to tell you about is Jennifer, the queen of the drama clique.

Oh, Jennifer!

Beautiful, beautiful Jennifer!

Stunning, unobtainable, stratospherically aloof Jennifer!

From the first instant I saw her, I knew I was either in love with her or terrified of her (I have trouble telling these two emotions apart). Either way, it made little difference, because even though she was in my class I was convinced that we'd never speak, and that she would never so much as notice my existence. For me to harbor any fantasy of approaching her was like an ant contemplating how to chat up a tiger, but just being able to occasionally look at her brightened my day.

Life, however, is full of surprises. Mostly bad ones, in my experience, but occasionally a beam of sunlight streaks out of the sky, picks you out, and says, "This is your lucky day!"

It happened in a drama class with Mr. Duverne, who, even though I found his classes excruciatingly uncomfortable, was the only teacher I actually liked. He was a tall, skinny black guy who always wore immaculate, crisp white shirts and had a voice that sounded like it was reciting romantic poetry even when he was actually telling you to tie your shoelaces. He found it impossible to teach a class without at some point using the phrase "When I was at the RSC with Glenda . . ." (RSC standing for Royal Shakespeare Company; Glenda being someone we were supposed to have heard of but hadn't.)

He usually made us warm up with an "improv exercise," where we'd be given a topic for a scene and told to act it out on the fly, making up our own lines as we went along. Unlike other teachers, he didn't let us choose who to work with but put us into groups himself. This was probably why I liked him. When you are the class spare part, "find yourself a partner" basically means "crawl into the corner and weep, you loser."

On the legendary day when Jennifer noticed my existence, the improv was on the topic of a couple discovering a secret that caused them to split up. By some miracle of good fortune and bad casting, Jennifer was paired with me.

"Okay, people!" said Mr. Duverne. "Find yourself a space and do some prep. I want it to be fresh—completely in the moment—so all you're doing here is planning out the scene, okay? Just getting the bare bones of the story. No rehearsing. I want the dialogue to come onstage. I want emotion. I want passion. This is a room where cliché comes to die. Now get to work."

I followed Jennifer to the side of the drama studio, my brain racing with instructions to myself: *Don't ogle! Don't stare too hard at her eyes or mouth. Don't look at anything below the neck, except maybe her feet! Don't go weird and silent! Be normal! Look at her normally!*

As Jennifer turned to me, I realized I suddenly had no recollection of how to arrange the muscles of my face. My mouth seemed to have been overtaken by an urge to grin, which could only be suppressed with heavy ongoing mental effort. As for what a mouth was supposed to do when it wasn't grinning, I no longer seemed to have any idea.

"You're the new guy?" she said.

"Yeah. Sam," I said, extending my arm for a handshake. *A handshake! What was I doing?! Since when do you shake hands with a classmate? Nooooooo! Backtrack!*

Before she could notice my gaffe, I extended my other

arm and tried to pass off the gesture as a warm-up stretch. I'm not sure she was convinced.

"I've been working on my crying," she said. "I want to use it in the scene, so it has to be you that dumps me, okay?"

"Um . . . is that . . . ?" I was about to say "plausible," but before the word came out I realized how desperate this would make me sound. "Um . . . yeah . . . Okay. That should work."

"So how about we start off lying down, like we're in bed or something . . ."

"In be—? *Kkkhhh khhhhhh.* Sorry. Something in my throat. It's nothing. Carry on."

" . . . and we wake up and you . . . like . . . go to the bathroom or something . . . and I roll over and find your phone . . . and there's some messages there from another woman."

"Another woman!? Oh, right. Yeah. I see. Yeah. That makes sense. Cool."

"Then we just go into a whole infidelity thing. Yeah? You think you can work with that?"

"Yeah. Cool. No problem."

"Listen, Mr. Duverne is seriously connected—agents, the whole bit—and he casts the school play, so we have to give this everything. Think of it as an audition."

"For what?"

"Just don't screw up."

"I'll try, but I'm not really . . . I mean, I'm not much of a . . ."

"ALL RIGHT, PEOPLE!" shouted Mr. Duverne. "Gather round! Let's keep the energy up and do this! Okay! So who wants to go first?"

Jennifer's hand shot into the air.

"Great! Jennifer and Sam. Off you go."

The class settled themselves on a scattered arc of chairs around a performance area that yawned ominously in front of me. Jennifer strode onstage and lay down. I froze at the edge.

Problem.

Not an actual physical problem. Not yet. But there were warning signs. Blood was heading south, and tension was mounting in my Socially Acceptable Behavior control room. *Don't get a boner!* I told myself. *Not in a drama class. Not onstage. Not in front of the whole class.*

Just. Don't.

"So we're . . . like . . . a couple? And it starts with us in bed," Jennifer announced.

Hearing the word "bed" spoken aloud, my Socially Acceptable Behavior control room raised the threat level to amber.

"No preamble," said Mr. Duverne.

Jennifer threw me a gritted-teeth get-on-with-it smile. I scurried to the stage area and lay down next to her. She closed her eyes.

Threat level red. Trouser Tent Warning Alarm about to sound.

"I'm supposed to be asleep. You have to start," she whispered.

I leaped up, desperate to get out of Jennifer's bed before biological catastrophe struck. Immediately after springing to my feet, I remembered I was supposed to be playing the part of a man waking from sleep, so I decided to account for my non-sleepy leap by saying, "God, I'm desperate for a piss."

This seemed like a clever idea in my head; less so when it came out of my mouth. As a ripple of sniggers rose up from the audience, Jennifer's still-closed eyes clenched with annoyance.

I hurried offstage. From the wings I saw her wake up, stretch extravagantly, roll onto her side, and pick up an imaginary phone. Her face froze. She poked the screen, her eyes bulging in their sockets. For a moment, she looked like she was suffering from a bout of constipation; then I realized she was attempting to cry. It looked like hard work.

When I felt like I'd given her weeping attempt a decent chance, I walked back onstage, saying, "Ah, that's better."

"WHAT'S THIS!?" she yelled.

"Um . . . a phone?"

"Who's Katrina?"

"Katrina?"

"Yes! Katrina! I've seen the messages."

"I . . . um . . ."

"How long have you been seeing her?"

"Um . . ."

"How *could* you?"

"I just . . . um . . ."

"After everything I've done for you? All these months standing by you! Helping you through rehab . . ."

"Rehab? Oh. Yeah. Rehab. It's been a tough time."

"How could you do that to me? Just cast me aside like a piece of used meat?"

She raised an arm and threw the imaginary phone at me.

"Ow! My face! That hit me!"

"I don't care. Why would you do that? What's wrong with you, Jacob?"

"Jacob? Oh. Jacob. I . . . um . . ."

"Is she the only one? Is she?"

"Um . . ."

Jennifer strode toward me, shoved me in the chest, and stepped so close that the Trouser Tent Warning Alarm began to honk noisily in my skull. "Tell me! I have to know!" she pleaded. Her constipation look was back, and one eyeball was beginning to moisten (though more in the manner of someone with hemorrhoids than someone suffering from heartbreak).

"Well . . . um . . . maybe there were a couple of others," I confessed.

"A couple?"

"Not at the same time. I'm not kinky or anything."

"You're a cheat and a liar! I never want to see you again. You think you can just trample on other people, but listen to me and listen to me good—I'm not your doormat! And I know exactly what will happen to you when I walk out of that door! You'll relapse right back to your bad old ways. You're weak. You're a weak man. I've been wasting my time on you . . . and you know what?"

"What?"

"If Katrina was here now, I'd thank her. Because she's shown me the man you really are. Goodbye, Jacob. Forever. I hope you get the life you deserve."

With that, she flounced out, marching straight through our imaginary bed and possibly also through a wall. Apart from that, she was exceptionally good at flouncing.

"Um . . . that's it," I said.

"Nice work, guys," said Mr. Duverne, over a short spatter

of applause. "Good emotion, Jennifer. Good power. And I thought your characterization was very convincing, Sam— out of your depth, terrified, tongue-tied in the face of feminine pride, with an edge of hollow bravado. Great. Who's next?"

Felipe's hand sprang up. He took the stage with a reluctant-looking Marina and immediately launched into an anguished monologue about how he was a high-flying lawyer with a gambling problem, and he owed "five g's" to a gangster who was going to turn up any minute and break his legs. He delivered this speech in an accent that began in New York before drifting, via Australia, to Wales.

"Um . . . how could this happen to us?" said Marina, her throat emitting a choking noise that sounded suspiciously like stifled laughter, followed by another that sounded like an attempt at a sob.

Felipe gave a very long response, which continued his vocal tour of the English-speaking world, culminating in breaking the news to Marina that he was leaving her and going into hiding in a Tibetan monastery, where he would be looking for a more spiritual approach to life and retraining as a tantric monk.

Marina did not appear to be as upset by this news as he wanted her to be. She was still trying to sob, but the laughter was now definitely winning.

When Felipe yelled petulantly, "YOU'RE SUPPOSED TO BE UPSET!" Mr. Duverne brought the improvisation to a close.

"How am I supposed to do this if she won't stay in character?" spluttered Felipe.

"What do you say to that, Marina?" asked Mr. Duverne.

"He's the one that came out of it, telling me I was supposed to be sad."

"That's what we agreed!"

"I was improvising," said Marina.

"No, you weren't."

"I was playing the part of a wife who thinks her husband's a massive bullshitter, and she's struggling not to laugh at him because she doesn't want to dent his fragile ego."

"Were you?" asked Mr. Duverne. "Or were you just having trouble keeping a straight face?"

"That too," conceded Marina.

"Okay," said Mr. Duverne. "Lots to think about there. Some room for improvement. Who's next?"

Felipe stamped back to his seat next to Jennifer, muttering something about Marina being "impossible to work with." Jennifer gave his arm a consoling stroke, and I overheard her whispering to him that he'd been "really intense."

When the bell went, I timed my exit from the classroom so that I went through the door just after Jennifer and set off alongside her on the way to the next class. Screwing up my courage, I said, "It was great improvising with you. Really interesting."

She shot me a look probably best described as withering, which is something she was extremely good at, because I genuinely did feel myself shrink under her gaze. She could do to me with one eyebrow what two weeks without water can do to a plant.

"You were amazing," I said, making one last-ditch attempt at a conversation.

She turned to face me, and the eyebrow went down again. A tiny flicker of interest flashed across her eyes.

"Really?" she said.

"Yeah."

"You think?"

"Yes! It was so convincing it felt like I was really there. I mean, I *was* really there, but it was like it was actually real."

"You thought I was good?"

"Incredible. I'm sorry I was kind of . . . I mean . . . I was trying my best but acting's not really my thing."

"You don't say. What *is* your thing?"

"Um . . . um . . . I used to be into soccer but . . . um . . . these days it's . . . what I'm really into is . . . I know a lot of guys like video games but personally . . . at the moment . . . I'd have to say my big passion is . . . reading. Books."

"Really? What kind of stuff?"

"What kind? Well . . . what I really like is . . . um . . . long ones."

"Long ones?"

"And short ones. Sometimes. But mainly long ones. They're more intense."

"Great," she said, with a flat, unconvinced intonation that included a distinct whiff of *I've been nice to you for almost a whole minute and now it's time for you to leave me alone.*

There was still some distance to go, but I sensed that my talking-to-girls skills were definitely improving.

Later that day, hanging out behind the bike racks with Jake during lunch hour, I was surprised to hear myself confessing some of what had been on my mind since the drama class. We didn't usually talk about this kind of thing, but I was overcome by the urge to give vent to the swirl of emotions coursing through me.

As we kicked the ball to and fro, I told him about the scene Jennifer and I had improvised together, and how powerful it was, and how we'd had a genuine actual conversation afterward.

He listened carefully, nodding his approval. "Wow!" he said. "You and Jennifer! And at the beginning you were actually in bed together?"

"Not a real bed. An imaginary bed. But yeah."

"Wow. Amazing!"

"It was."

"Yeah."

"So now I'm kind of wondering . . . what should I do next?"

"In what sense?" he asked.

"Now that she's talking to me, how do I . . . you know . . . move things forward."

"Hang on. Are you . . . ?"

"What?"

Jake now had a disbelieving smirk on his face. "You're not . . . ?"

"What?"

The smirk was now turning into a smile. "You don't mean you're actually thinking . . . you and Jennifer . . . ?"

This is when the smile became a laugh. I decided to backtrack.

"No," I said. "Not like that. I just meant as friends."

"You and Jennifer!"

He was still laughing.

"Not in that way. I didn't mean it like that."

Still laughing. Louder now. Actually clutching his sides.

"You . . . hahaha . . . I'm   sorry . . . hahaha . . . you   actually . . . hahaha . . . I think I'm choking." He was now on the ground, in the fetal position, struggling for breath. "JENNIFER! . . . AND YOU! . . . Amazing! . . . I'm sorry . . . I'm sorry . . ."

When I began to think he might never stop I decided to leave. If he suffocated to death, alone behind the bike racks, it would be his own fault.

Sometimes the only way to salvage your dignity is to walk away. Ideally you'd do this before your dignity has been battered to a soggy, flattened pulp, but timing was never my strong point.

My first (and probably last) pottery class

By the end of the day, my confidence still hadn't recovered from Jake's less-than-supportive response to my confession. I was desperate to get away from school as fast as possible, but someone had to walk Freya home, and following a painful ten-minute wait in the playground after final bell, she still hadn't appeared.

Ethan was sitting on a low wall with a group of three senior girls from the asymmetric haircuts/too-cool-to-try-to-look-pretty-but-hugely-foxy-anyway clique. He had his arms around two of them. They were locked in a private, semi-whispered conversation.

In Stevenage, Ethan had been an outsider, always on the edge of things, with a tiny number of friends who I always suspected he didn't even like. Now, suddenly, he was The Man and I was the outcast.

I'd always thought these things were decided on some kind of objective scale, and that if you were relatively normal you'd probably stay that way, but now I'd learned (the hard way) that if you changed schools, you could end up in an environment where everything you thought you knew about the world turned out to be wrong.

If I took a step back from the situation and tried to think things through rationally, I could see that the North London Academy for the Gifted and Talented was a unique and freakish place, which meant that to be a misfit here didn't make me abnormal, but logic is of limited use up against the reality of being surrounded every day by people who simply don't like you. The fact that I didn't like them just as much as they didn't like me wasn't much comfort.

Ethan, meanwhile, was having the time of his life.

I knew he wouldn't want me to interrupt his flirty snuggle, but I was desperate to leave and I guessed he couldn't be too obnoxious to me in front of his hot friends, so I walked over and said, "Are you waiting for Freya, or do I have to?"

The circle of girls peeled open.

"This is my kid brother," said Ethan, in a much less sneery tone of voice than I'd anticipated.

"Awww," said the one with a nose stud. "He's sweet."

"I know," said Ethan.

YOU KNOW!? my inner voice screamed. *YOU*

KNOW!? YOU'VE NEVER CALLED ME SWEET IN YOUR LIFE! AND I'M NOT SWEET!

"Ah, he's blushing," said the one with a red streak dyed into her dark bangs.

"I'm only two years younger than him!" I snapped, more snappily than I'd intended. "Our feet are almost the same size."

"TMI!" said Ethan, waggling a hand in my direction. The girls laughed, one of them slapping him affectionately on the chest as she did so.

"Who's walking Freya home?" I said, attempting to press on through the unsettling sensation of knowing I was being laughed at and having no idea why.

"You. I'm hanging out here for a bit. Catching up on the gossip."

I gave him a *who are you?/what's happened to you?* look, but he didn't appear to notice. Or care. *Gossip?* Since when did he *gossip?*

As I was trying to think of a cutting riposte, Freya sprinted up to me, handed over three still-wet paintings, her schoolbag, and a coat, and immediately launched into a gabbled story about one of her pictures being selected for inclusion in the school newsletter, how this happened, the subject of the drawing, the story behind the subject for the drawing, etc.

Talking to Freya doesn't require much talking. Nodding is merely optional. Even staying awake is less than essential. We walked home, side by side, Freya narrating, me daydreaming wistful and inappropriate thoughts about Ethan's friends.

I was hungry when I got home, bordering on hangry, but there was no sign of Mom, so I went down the garden to the duck-egg blue "studio" to find her. I still didn't believe anything that color could possibly come out of a bird's ass.

Twangy sitar music was playing and the air was thick with pungent incense smoke, which had an aroma halfway between hard candy and unwashed armpit. Mom was standing at her potter's wheel, wearing her clay-smeared arty-farty smock, her hair tucked away under a lurid bandanna.

"Hello, darling," she said. "I'm just throwing."

"Up?"

"Up what?"

"You're throwing up?"

"I'm throwing a pot."

The wheel was spinning at high speed. A shiny cone of wet clay, under gentle pressure from her fingertips, was developing new ripples and curves, bending outward at the rim. It was mesmerizing to watch, so much so that I temporarily forgot I was hungry. This *never* happens. Up until this moment, the only thing that had ever stopped me from feeling hungry was eating. And even that sometimes didn't work.

"Can I try?" I asked.

"This?"

"Yeah. It looks cool."

Mom stopped the wheel and pried off the clay with a long spatula. She placed her half-finished pot on a shelf and smiled at me nervously, her face wearing a base layer of suspicion and reluctance overlaid with a brittle veneer of maternal encouragement.

"Really? You want to make a pot?"

"Yeah."

With an open palm, she gestured me onto her stool, showed me how to control the speed of the wheel with a foot pedal, then handed me a lump of wet clay.

"Aim for the middle or it has a tendency to . . ."

I pumped the accelerator and tossed down the clay, hard. It landed off-center, went around a couple of times, then flew off and stuck to the wall.

". . . fly off," said Mom, peeling the clay from the now-significantly-less-duck-egg-blue wall. "Gently, now," she said, handing me back the gooey brown lump.

"Not too fast. Aim for the middle," she added, using the tone of voice parents have when they're trying to be patient with you and give you the benefit of the doubt, but they know you're not listening and they're actually already angry with you for the thing you haven't done yet, but which you both know is about to happen.

I pressed down with my foot, tossed the clay, around around around, flinnggg . . . splat!

"Hey! This is great!" I said.

Who knew pottery could be so much fun?

"All right," said Mom, peeling the clay from another freshly stained spot on the studio wall. "This is your last chance. Easy on the speed. *Gentle* toss right into the middle. Do you know what the word 'gentle' means?"

I set the wheel to a slow, sedate rotation. I clutched the wet ball of clay in my hands. I took aim. Then, at the last second, I couldn't help myself. Right down on the pedal. Big hard chuck. Around around around . . . *shwinnggg* . . . *wheee* . . . straight toward the window . . . crash! . . . and out into the garden.

Amazingly, I managed not to laugh. I think I may have had a big grin on my face though. Which was unwise.

"You did that on purpose!"

"I didn't."

"I told you to set it slow."

"My foot slipped."

"No, it didn't."

"I couldn't help myself. Sorry."

"Aaargggghhh! Why do you have to be like this!?"

"Like what?"

"You're just so . . . *male*."

"Is that a bad thing?"

"You can't resist being too rough and pushing everything to the limit and breaking things!"

"I didn't mean to."

"Given the choice, you'd rather smash something than make something, wouldn't you?"

I wasn't smiling anymore. I felt my face draining of blood, as if she'd slapped me, and I turned away so she wouldn't see.

She tried to put a hand on my shoulder, but I shrugged her off and walked away. Her voice pursued me up the garden. "Sorry. I didn't mean that. Darling! I was just upset. That sounded all wrong. Sam! Stop! I didn't mean any of that. You're very creative. You just need a bit more direction than . . . I mean . . . You're a very physical boy. You're active with your body, and that's a great thing. We all have different talents."

At the back door, I stopped and turned to face her.

"No we don't."

"Of course we do," she said, extending a hand toward me again.

"What's so great about talent?" I said, stepping out of reach. "Why does everyone have to be *talented*? Because if everyone's talented, then nobody is. Why can't I just be normal?"

"Is that what you want?"

"It's not what I *want*. It's what I *am*. What I want is for everyone to stop acting like this makes me some kind of weirdo."

And with that I flounced off. It was a damn good flounce too. So I had learned something in school that day.

I couldn't forget what she'd said though. That night, and the next day, and the day after that, our argument kept replaying itself in my head. She'd tried to backtrack, but there was no way for her to unsay what had slipped out. She saw Ethan and Freya as creative and me as destructive. She admired their imagination and thought I had no ideas of my own. It wasn't just at school that I was somehow substandard; it was at home too. Even my own mom seemed to think I was a failure.

Was this what she really thought of me? Was I a disappointment to her? Had she said things she didn't mean in an outburst of temper, or had anger pushed aside her tactful lies and revealed a hidden truth?

Then it occurred to me there was a way to find out. Her blog.

How to cyberstalk your mother

I started by trying to look on Mom's laptop, but she'd changed the password and developed the habit of logging out when she left it unattended (which proved straight off that she didn't trust me). Then I remembered that I'd overheard her chatting to friends about her "creative modern mom" blog, and with a flash of inspiration, the idea came to me of googling this phrase, along with Mom's name, on my phone.

And up it popped. Her blog. My life. For anyone to see.

Just the sight of it—seeing her name and a cheesy photo at the top, over an embarrassing fake-parchment background scattered with clip-art candles and stars—gave me the creeps. The whole thing was so clunkily designed it looked like it was put online about ten minutes after the internet was invented.

The title of the latest post was "Interesting Times and Fresh Challenges." I knew instinctively there was nothing to be gained by reading it. I knew it would either annoy or upset me, or both.

So, obviously, I read it.

Interesting times and fresh challenges in our creative North London household. Children can be so adaptable . . . yet so conservative. You never know what is around the next corner!

My eldest and youngest continue to embrace our transformed unconventional lifestyle, thriving and growing, discovering new talents, capacities, and passions. Anyone who read my last post (thank you for all your messages of support and encouragement—so many tears and so much bravery and joy) cannot fail to have been moved by how the fresh, liberated environment of our new life has at last given E____ the confidence to embrace his sexuality.

That he has been unable to open up his true self until now almost breaks my heart. Thank God we made the change when we did, before repression and self-denial sank deeper tendrils into his soul.

But while E____ and F____ are responding with open hearts and minds to our new ethos, S____ is still digging his heels in. Our sudden openness seems to make him feel insecure, and he appears threatened by my role as an independent creative being. We had a particularly revealing encounter in my studio recently. I usually hide my creative process from the children, not wanting them to feel jealous. (Yes, my pottery work does occasionally feel like another child! Equally rewarding, equally challenging!) But on this occasion, S___ walked in while I was mid-throw.

To my surprise, he seemed genuinely interested and asked if he could try. This struck me as a positive step, so I handed him some clay and encouraged him to express himself.

"Why didn't I think of this before?" I even thought. "Perhaps this will be the key to unlocking his inhibited and resistant persona!"

How foolish of me. I could hardly have been more wrong.

He approached the clay—that small, infinitely precious parcel of Mother Earth itself—with shocking brutality and anger, almost as if he had found an objective correlative for the negative emotions he has been feeling for me, his own mother.

Time and again, he accelerated the wheel to a vicious and inappropriately violent speed, then launched the clay with undisguised antagonism in such a way that it struck the wheel and flew off, against the wall, and ultimately through a window, shattering the glass.

This wordless articulation of his negative emotions could hardly have been more stark or clear. I tried to encourage him to talk to me about these feelings, but he shrugged me off and withdrew.

Such eloquence with the language of clay! Such difficulty with the language of words! If only he would stop fighting me, I could help him. But how to achieve this . . . ?

Well, dear friends of the online mothering blog community, I have looked to you for support, and you haven't failed me. Courtesy of the wise, humane, and inspirational Alanisette Spink and her brilliant "RightBackAtchaSon" blog, I have hit upon the idea of the "Love Bomb" approach.

I'm going to try this on S___, to see if it works. The more anger he throws at me, the more love I will hurl back. I will neutralize negativity with the force of relentless patience and goodwill. Check out Alanisette's "Off-Roading with Angry Teenagers" for a fuller account of the method.

We'll see where this gets me. There may be a few more smashed windows along the way . . .

Fingers crossed!

One last thing: calendula toothpaste is a marvel! Big Pharma has us all hooked on the monster drug, fluoride, but not in this household. Fight the good fight, sisters!

At first, I didn't know what to say or do or think. My mom was out of her mind! None of this made any sense. I hadn't smashed the window because I was angry. *She's* the one who was angry! I was having a laugh, seeing what happened if you set the wheel to max speed. I mean, what kind of person could try one of those things and not pump down on the accelerator?

But now I *was* angry. How could she write this about me—getting everything so utterly wrong—and put it up online for anyone to read?

I couldn't just take this lying down and let her get away with it.

But instead of confronting her, an alternative plan began to take shape in my mind. I googled "RightBackAtchaSon," and "Off-Roading with Angry Teenagers" came up right away. The home page was emblazoned with an image of a woman in a pair of large but alarmingly tight salmon-pink shorts, embracing two scowling, cap-on-backward boys, pictured in front of a car the size of a small house. Her blog mainly seemed to be a moan about how horrible they were (which was very plausible) and an explanation of why this was not her fault (which wasn't).

The "Love Bomb" method seemed to be based on the theory that children misbehave when they feel they are unloved, and stated that if, for a short period of time, you go out of your way to satisfy all their needs and desires, however irrational or demanding, it will dawn on them that they *are* loved, and their behavior will improve.

This was interesting.

Very interesting indeed.

If Mom really was planning to Love Bomb me—to satisfy all my needs and desires, however irrational or demanding—well, the possibilities were endless.

I decided to go downstairs and try an experiment.

The kitchen was filled with the smell of boiling whole-grain rice and steamed purple-sprouting broccoli.

"God, I'd love a burger," I said.

Mom turned to me and frowned. She then froze for a moment and corrected her expression to a plastic TV-commercial smile.

"I'm making a nice healthy dinner with a low GI but maybe you could have some chocolate afterward."

"I *wish* I could have a burger. We could order takeout. You always used to say it was too expensive, but we can afford it now, can't we? Oh, come on. A burger! I want a burger *sooooo* much! With ketchup and bacon and jack cheese and fries on the side! Oh God, I can picture it!"

"That kind of food gives a hollow surge of directionless energy, followed by an inevitable crash. It's really bad for you."

What did it take to kick the Love Bomb into action? Did I need to start shouting? Weeping?

"Please! It's the only thing I want in the whole world!"

I could almost see the cogs in Mom's brain whirring.

She sighed deeply, then said, "Well, okay. Just this once. If it's really important to you."

"Yes! Yes! Thank you, thank you!"

And thank *you*, Alanisette Spink. I ran out of the room to get Mom's iPad, and within minutes a round of burgers was on the way.

This was unprecedented. Mom surrendering with barely a struggle in the face of her worst enemy—junk-food takeout—was conclusive proof that she really was doing the Love Bomb.

Which gave me an interesting challenge. How long could I keep this going? If I was too nice or happy, she might think it had worked and would cancel the program. If I was too rude or grumpy, she might write it off as a failure and abandon it.

There was a fine line to be walked. I would find it though. Oh yes, I would find it.

When Mom asked me, with glistening puppy-dog eyes, if I'd enjoyed my burger, I just said, "Yup," which felt about right. Rude and ungrateful enough to make me seem troubled, but not so much that she might want to give up on me.

For a moment, as I mopped up the last blobs of ketchup and meat juice from my plate, I kind of hated myself for being a brat, but, on the other hand, any teenager who passed up an opportunity like this without latching on an industrial milking machine and sucking it dry would be certifiably insane.

This burger, I realized, was just the beginning. It was time to fire up the heavy-duty pumps and see what would happen.

A social life that isn't social. Or a life

Although I had made the breakthrough and achieved an actual conversation with Jennifer, she and her drama clique remained as unapproachable as ever. They always moved around the school in a tight huddle, like a group of chattering emperor penguins getting through a hostile winter using shared body heat and the warming power of snarky gossip.

They had the unnerving habit of suddenly all bursting into laughter at the same moment, producing a chorus of squeals, cackles, and snorts that made everyone else in the room spin around to see if they were the person being laughed at.

I can't really say I was ostracized, because if what it takes to be "in" is to hang out with someone like Felipe, trading anecdotes about what your fencing teacher said to you the other day, then . . . well . . . it doesn't even occur to you to be anything other than "out." (That's fencing with swords, not putting up fences, in case you were wondering.)

My only company was Jake and our aimless kickabouts behind the bike racks at the back of the staff parking lot. It had never been a particularly talkative friendship, and since the Jennifer conversation it had become more non-verbal than ever, but as long as you have soccer, that's okay.

This wasn't the social life anyone outside of a prison would choose, but it was better than nothing. Marginally.

After a stray kick broke the side-view mirror of Mrs. Florizel's car, resulting in our ball being confiscated, we continued to meet up during lunch, but I had the feeling that neither of us quite knew why.

Then, out of the blue, he told me he was leaving. His dad had been laid off, so they were sending him to a public school. At the end of the week.

"With no warning?" I stammered. "Just like that?"

"It happened a while ago."

"The sacking? Or you deciding to leave?"

"Both. I just didn't want to tell you."

"Why not?"

"I thought you'd be upset. You know—because you don't have any other friends."

"Yes I do!"

"Who?"

"Um . . . maybe not at school, but I do in other places!"

"That's what I meant."

"Anyway, *you* don't have any other friends either," I retorted.

"I know. That's why I suggested saving money by taking me out of here."

"It was your idea?"

"Yeah. Sorry."

He couldn't look at me. His eyes remained fixed guiltily on his feet, where a soccer ball would have been if we'd had one.

"I don't blame you," I said eventually. "I'd do the same if I could. Maybe I need to think of a way to bankrupt my dad."

"Sorry," he said again. "You're a nice guy and everything, but I just can't handle it here."

"What am I going to do when you're gone?"

"I dunno. Maybe you'll have to find a way to . . . kind of . . . join in."

"You serious?"

"It's either that or get a switchblade and take up smoking with Psycho Steve."

"I can't believe this has happened to me. I used to be popular."

"Me too."

"I used to be normal."

"Me too."

"I'll miss you," I said.

He nodded in response, which might have been a way to say that he'd miss me too, but it was hard to be sure.

The bell went and we drifted back to class. For the rest of the week I avoided the bike racks. I didn't even know if he was there. The whole thing seemed too depressing.

Now I really was alone.

My hollow victory

At first, the loss of my only school friend was made up for by the milking of the Love Bomb at home. I had never eaten so much junk food in my life. Chips and chocolate rained down. Bedtime was only half-heartedly enforced. I gorged on TV.

In the strangest turn of events yet, Mom even did a U-turn on the one thing she hated even more than take-out meals: video games. This victory began with Mom appearing behind me while I was enjoying a spot of lethal hand-to-hand combat in *Call of Duty*.

"What are you doing?" she said, not in the turn-off-that-disgusting-filth tone she normally used when I was gaming, but in a trying-to-take-an-interest-in-my-son's-bizarre-and-distressingly-violent-hobbies voice, which I had never heard before.

The idea that she might be attempting to Love Bomb my most gory video game was too much. It was all wrong. If she stopped hating video games, I wouldn't know who she was any more.

"Killing stuff! It's great! Watch this!" I said. I wasn't going to make this easy for her.

I took out a grenade and blew a Nazi's head off. "See that!" I enthused. "Splatted him!"

From the reflection of her face in the TV screen I could see that I had already cured her of any desire to Love Bomb the PlayStation.

"How long have you been playing?" she said, returning us straight back to our usual video game conversation.

"I dunno."

"Don't you think that's enough screen time for one day?"

"Not really."

"I want you to switch it off."

"Why?"

This was more like it. Normal service resumed.

"Can you at least pause it while I'm trying to talk to you?"

I paused the game but didn't stop staring at the screen.

"Don't you have any homework?" she asked.

"Done it."

"You were only in your room half an hour."

"It's a slacker school. Your choice."

"Can't you find something creative to do?"

"Like what?"

"Anything."

"Anyway, this *is* creative. Do you know how many ways there are to kill people?" (I knew I shouldn't wind her up, but it was just too tempting. Sometimes she made it so easy it's like she was actually begging me to annoy her.)

"You sound sick in the head when you talk like that," she replied, taking the bait, even though she knew it was bait. We both knew how this conversation went, following a long-established ritual pattern, a bit like sumo wrestling.

"If that's what you think, then half the kids in the world are psychos, 'cause everyone does it!"

"No they don't. Ethan and Freya never had the slightest interest."

"Oh, here we go. Ethan and Freya. Wonderful Ethan and Freya! Same old shit!"

I unpaused the game and chucked a couple more grenades. Mom stepped toward me and snatched the controller from my hands. We stared at each other in hostile silence, to a soundtrack of battleground carnage. After a while, someone leaped out of a hole in the ground and slit my throat. On-screen, that is. In real life things remained pretty tense but no actual homicide was attempted.

"I don't like the way our relationship is going," said Mom eventually. "I've been trying to make things better, but I don't think you've noticed."

I shrugged.

"I think we need to talk more," she said.

"The opposite might work better. Maybe we should talk less."

"Please don't hate me," said Mom. "I'm sorry. I shouldn't compare you to Ethan and Freya. You're you, and that's great, and you shouldn't think I want you to be like them."

"That's exactly what you do think," I said, making eye contact with her for the first time, holding her gaze for a moment, then standing up and stepping toward the door.

"No!" said Mom, reaching out an arm to block my path. "When I said that about Ethan and Freya I wasn't comparing you to them."

"Yes you were."

"All three of you are different, and that's great. I don't want you to be anyone other than who you are."

"Yeah, right."

"Please don't think that!"

I sensed a hug looming, and angled my shoulders to impede her approach. She was looking slightly teary, which was kind of alarming.

103

"I'm sorry you're unhappy at school," she said, "but everything will work out for you in the end if you stop fighting it. We came down here and started a new life so you could all be happier."

"Not me. If you wanted me to be happy we would have stayed in Stevenage."

"Trust me. Everything will get better soon. I love you."

She began to rub my back, which felt simultaneously comforting and deeply awkward. After a while, she said, "Okay—if it's important to you to play more video games, play more video games. If that's what makes you happy."

I shrugged, sat down, and started a new game. It was a while before Mom turned and left.

Objectively, this was a major victory, but it felt hollow. I couldn't tell if her screen-time concession was part of the Love Bomb strategy, or something else. Weirdly, I found myself unable to focus, and soon got killed by a blood-splattered man who jumped through the window, knifed me in the leg, then torched me with a flamethrower. (In the game, that is. Just to be clear.)

After that, I switched off.

Fight! Fight! Fight!

My first Social Outcast Concealment Strategy after Jake left was to try appearing aloof. You don't need a switchblade and a cloud of cancerous smoke to be aloof. They help, sure, but I could at least try without them. I thought if I wandered around looking indifferent and superior, as if I inhabited a private interior world far more fascinating than anything mere friends could offer, maybe I wouldn't seem like a total loser.

Unfortunately, I wasn't very good at indifferent, and I was completely hopeless at superior. You need a certain confident-and-dark bearing, but I was born with one of those faces that makes me look like I want to be your friend. Without the heavy use of either latex or plastic surgery, there's nothing I can do about it, so my attempt at aloof was a total failure.

I was at least beginning to find the classes less freakish. You get used to anything eventually, and I'd learned that, as with any other school, if you kept your head down and turned in passable work, teachers would always be too occupied with the attention-seeking kids to give you much grief. So it turned out that perhaps I did belong in a gifted and talented school after all, my personal aptitude being a talent for blending into the background.

Sometimes I felt resigned to my level of invisibility, to drifting from class to class like a ghost, to living without friends or enemies and dragging myself aimlessly through evenings and weekends without even really knowing how I was making the time pass; at other times I felt my life was slipping away. Ethan's and Freya's friends were constantly coming and going through our house, and they both always seemed to be rushing from place to place, struggling to fit complex social plans into the matrix of their week, while I had endless empty hours to fill.

To make matters worse, instead of subtly milking the Love Bomb and keeping the supply flowing, in a moment of bored and thoughtless stupidity I crashed into Mom's bedroom while she was working on her blog and told her I wasn't getting enough pocket money.

She looked up from her laptop, narrowed her eyes, and asked me in a steely voice to repeat what I'd just said.

I immediately sensed that I'd caught her in the wrong mood. "I . . . um . . . I was just talking about it with my friends at school," I said, "and it turns out they all get about ten times as much as me. I mean, things are different in London, aren't they? Cost of living and all that. And I was wondering if . . . if . . . it's just I feel really left out when everyone else is doing stuff I can't afford. That's all. It's not a big thing."

My milking skills had reached a very high level of proficiency since the start of the Love Bomb, but this was a major fumble.

I smiled sweetly at her (with a hint of tragic bravery), but she kept up her weary-cop-examining-a-bag-of-incriminating-evidence face.

"Which friends? What stuff?" she asked.

"Oh, nothing in particular."

"Who's leaving you out of what?"

"It's nothing specific. I just thought I'd stand a better chance of fitting in at school if I was getting the same pocket money as the other people in my class."

"Who all get ten times more than you?"

"Yeah."

"You want me to multiply your pocket money by *ten*?"

"No. Not necessarily. I mean . . . double would be fine."

"Fine?"

"Generous, I mean. It's just a suggestion."

"You came in here to *suggest* that I double your pocket money?"

I knew this was going badly. I should have bailed out, but instead, toying clumsily with the wires of the Love Bomb detonator, heedless of the imminent peril, I turned up the pressure. "I just thought . . . I mean . . . I've been having a lot of negative emotions recently . . . and challenges with . . . destructive energies that are . . ." My eyes may have flicked unwittingly toward the screen of her laptop, looking for inspiration, because Mom suddenly interrupted me.

"Have you been reading my blog?"

Only now did I realize what I'd done. It was too late to backtrack.

"No," I said.

Mom's eyes clouded over. I knew this was the end.

"You read that thing about the Love Bomb, didn't you?"

"No . . . I mean, what love bomb? What's a love bomb?"

"And you've been milking me ever since."

"Milking? What an . . . outrageous . . . I . . . I don't even like milk."

I'm no expert in legal cross-examination, but I knew this was weak.

"That's what all this pocket-money-and-junk-food

emotional bribery is about, isn't it? You've been taking me for a ride!"

"A ride?"

"How *could* you? Here I am, trying everything I can to make you happier, and you just use it as a trick to get burgers and cash!"

Put like that, it didn't sound great. I countered with everything I could think of in my own defence, which amounted to, "I . . . um . . ."

That was it.

Mom stared at me coldly. "How could you be so calculating?"

"I was just . . . I mean . . . I like burgers."

"I'm trying to love you the best I can."

This was going too far now. She was leading me into territory where I could not go. Basic self-preservation survival instincts were beginning to kick in, yelling at me to vacate the area as soon as possible or pay a heavy price.

"Sorry," I said.

"I can't help you if you won't help yourself. I can't begin to make things better for you if you continue to be so totally determined to hate London and hate your school and make no effort at all to fit in and enjoy all the opportunities you have here. You have to stop being so negative. You're pushing everyone away."

"I'm not pushing anyone away."

"You really are, Sam. Family, friends, everyone. You're determined to be stuck in the past, and that's only ever going to make you miserable. You need to have a serious think about whether you want to keep on being this person."

"Okay. I'll go and do that now," I said, taking this as an opportunity to make an exit without it seeming like I was running away. Or at least without it seeming too obvious that I was running away. Okay, it *was* obvious I was running away, but that's just what had to happen. I had to get out of there.

I went to my room, and I did have a think, but not a very productive one. Thinking is hard. Especially on the subject of what you've done wrong. Before you know it, instead of mulling over ways to be more considerate to your family, you're imagining scoring a hat trick for Barcelona. With Jennifer cheering you on from the stands. Then driving her back home to a penthouse apartment, having a cocktail or two together, and . . . anyway, before you know it your mind has strayed on to a very different topic.

Some people have focused, polite brains like obedient white poodles that never get dirty and obey every command their owners issue. My brain is more like some filthy mutt who runs off and scrabbles through trash cans without even caring that it's being shouted at to come to heel.

And like a dog returning triumphantly to its owner with a rotting, discarded sausage in its jaws, the only identifiable idea my brain dredged up was that I was a useless, uninteresting, and average person, destined to spend the rest of my life on the periphery, watching other people have all the fun.

Did I want to be this person? No. But that's who I was, and I couldn't think of any way to change it.

This feeling was brought into even sharper focus by a strange encounter after school the following day. I was used to being ignored by everyone in my class, so at first I didn't know how to respond when, emerging into the playground on my way home, I was enthusiastically hailed by Felipe.

"Hey! Sam! Come here! I want to talk to you," he called, summoning me with a wave of the hand.

I paused, contemplating my options. He was perched on a low wall, surrounded by the rest of the drama clique, wearing a smile that looked halfway between friendly and predatory.

"Come here!" he repeated. "I want to ask you something."

If Jennifer hadn't been there I probably would have just walked on, claiming to be in a hurry, but even though I sensed it wouldn't end well, even though I knew I was making a mistake, I asked what he wanted.

"I've been meaning to say for ages that I thought the improv you did with Jennifer . . . the one about you having lots of girlfriends at the same time . . . it was really good. It was powerful stuff," he said. His voice and facial expression were utterly sincere, but out of the corner of my eye I could see his gaggle of followers smirking.

"Thanks," I replied, turning away.

"Wait, wait! Don't rush off! Did you know the auditions for the school play are next week? You should go for it. Really."

A couple of smirks turned into audible sniggers. I began to walk toward the school gates, but he jumped up and put a hand on my shoulder, stopping me.

"Wait! Don't be like that! Honestly—I thought you were really good."

"Fine. I have to go."

"Don't. We need you for something."

"What?"

"To resolve a bet."

"What bet?"

"It's just . . . we were talking about that improv . . . you know, where you played Jennifer's boyfriend—really convincingly—and some of us thought you got a bit . . . overenthusiastic. I mean it's hard to tell with such a good actor, isn't it? So there's a bet going. About whether you like her."

"Felipe!" snapped Jennifer, leaping toward him and hitting him on the chest, then turning to me and adding, "Ignore him. He's just messing with you."

I couldn't help noticing that after hitting him, Jennifer's hand stayed where it was, touching Felipe's chest.

I'm not an angry person. Not usually. I have a pretty calm demeanor, on the whole. But at this moment, the urge to punch Felipe in the face was almost overwhelming. Unfortunately, he was almost twice my size. Not in terms of height, but sheer bulk. Felipe had a gym body, with broad shoulders and proper man-muscles always bulging and twitching through his flesh-hugging clothes. My body was essentially that of a twelve-year-old who has been stretched to an implausible and ungainly length in a freakish experiment gone horribly wrong. Unless the experiment was an attempt to create a living stick figure, in which case it had gone horribly right.

Punching, in short, wasn't an option. But I knew I couldn't walk away either. I had to stand my ground. I couldn't let myself shrink any further into invisibility. I couldn't let Felipe humiliate and belittle me in front of so many people, with Jennifer at his side watching me shrivel.

So instead of meekly slipping home, defeated, I squared up to Felipe and said, "You've guessed wrong. It's you I like. Every time I see you in your white jeans with your little peach-fuzz goatee I get a boner. If you didn't spend every lunch hour admiring yourself in the mirror, you would have noticed."

A ripple of shocked laughter rose up from the clique behind him.

Felipe's mouth pursed and his eyelids twitched. I could see his mind whirring. Our conversation had taken a turn he wasn't expecting.

"That's a complete lie!" he said. "Specially coming from someone who clearly doesn't look in a mirror, like, *ever*!" He delivered this line as if it was a brilliant pearl of devastating wit, but nobody laughed, perhaps because nobody noticed it was even supposed to be a joke.

"Where did you come from, anyway?" he added eventually, after a long, effortful think. "Did you get expelled from some other school for being too much of a nerd?"

"No. My family moved to London."

"Where from? Nerdland?" he said triumphantly, laughing at his second attempt at humor, which fell even flatter than the first.

"Stevenage," I said, sensing that giving his stupid questions sensible answers was the best way to help him look like even more of an idiot.

"Hah! Same thing! Where is that, anyway?"

"North of London."

"Eee oop! Our kid's from the North! I'll bet ya feend it rit funny doon here. Electricity. Inside toilets. Does oor Sam find it scary doon in the big city?"

"You have no idea where the North even is, do you?"

"Why would I want to?"

"And since you ask, I don't find London scary, but I do have trouble with some of the arrogant, brain-dead jackoffs you meet down here, who think they're God's gift just because they've got a rich daddy. That's a big change."

A couple of people behind Felipe laughed. Someone actually let out one of those playground "Ooohs" that means "You're not going to let him say that, are you?"

The air between us seemed to thicken. I glanced over Felipe's shoulder and for an instant met Jennifer's gaze. She was wide-eyed, staring right at me, clearly as amazed by my chutzpah as Felipe, but, unlike him, she seemed to be smiling.

For a second or two after seeing Jennifer's reaction, I felt a surge of the kind of joy and adrenaline you must get when you leap out of a plane at the start of a parachute jump, during those first weightless, liberated moments before you remember that you have to land.

Felipe—who wasn't a great wit—eventually responded by shoving me in the chest and saying, "Are you talking about me?"

The force of his shove pushed me back a couple of steps, but when I regained my balance I didn't retreat any further.

"Are you?" he repeated.

I could easily have run away—it was the obvious thing to do at this point—but as I stood there, watching him approach for another shove, I saw a flicker of doubt in his eyes, which told me that despite his size and swagger and bulging muscles, this was a soft rich kid who had never been in a fight in his life. His chest and chin might have been jutting out in a display of macho confidence, but I could sense, with my old Stevenage instincts, that he was terrified of taking even a single punch.

I'd never personally been in a fight either, but I at least knew what a fight was, and was less afraid of the whole scenario than him. And if you're less afraid, you've kind of won.

So I replied, quite calmly, "Yes. I am talking about you."

As I said those words, I realized that I was now taking my place in the long and noble history of men getting into fights to impress girls. Okay, so maybe the word "noble" doesn't really belong there—"stupid" might be more fitting—but I sensed myself stepping up, manning up, and I still (perhaps due to some defect in my mental wiring) felt no fear. In fact, I felt strangely elated. Only yesterday, Mom had told me that the path to happiness was to let myself change and embrace new experiences. Now I was putting this into practice, and already it seemed to be working.

This probably wasn't what she had in mind, but it was definitely a start.

More "Ooohs" rose from Felipe's gang, who had all now gotten up from the wall and were gathered around us.

The magnetic pull of an imminent fight must have been felt across the playground, because we were soon surrounded by a crowd of spectators who left a patch of space around us roughly the size of a boxing ring. Felipe looked utterly befuddled, almost punch-drunk, which seemed a little premature.

That age-old chant began to rise up around us: "Fight! Fight! Fight!"

For one lovely moment, I felt almost as if I was back at my old school. The thought that, despite all the superficial differences, children and teenagers everywhere were essentially the same wrapped itself around me like a warm, fluffy blanket.

Then something bizarre happened. Suddenly, Felipe and I weren't alone in the ring. A small girl was in there with us. It was Freya, and she kicked off the fight early, punching Felipe in the stomach and yelling, "YOU LEAVE HIM ALONE, YOU BIG HAIRY BULLY! YOU SHOULD BE ASHAMED OF YOURSELF! IF YOU MESS WITH HIM YOU MESS WITH ME AND I SWEAR TO GOD IF YOU LAY ONE FINGER ON MY BIG BROTHER I'LL FIND OUT WHERE YOU LIVE AND I'LL COME AND KILL YOU IN THE NIGHT WHILE YOU'RE SLEEPING."

Felipe flinched under her blows, deflecting most of them, unable to get a word in edgewise. Soon, nothing she said was audible anyway, since every single spectator was collapsing with laughter.

"ALL RIGHT! THAT'S IT! WE'RE GOING HOME!" said Freya, taking my hand and leading me out through the circle of spectators. I was too stunned to do anything but go with her.

Behind us, the sound of laughter slowly subsided as the crowd began to dissolve.

Ethan intercepted us at the school gates. "That wasn't you, was it?" he said. "In the middle of that fight?"

"Yeah. It was."

"Who with?"

"Felipe."

"Felipe? The big guy with the stupid little beard?"

"Yeah."

"He was bullying Sam!" said Freya.

"Is that true?" asked Ethan.

I shrugged.

"You have to report him," he said.

"No need," said Freya. "I've dealt with it."

"*I've* dealt with it," I said. "It's fine. I'm not afraid of him."

Ethan gave me a thoughtful stare, like the one Mom gives when she's trying to figure out what I'm hiding. "I've got band practice," he said, more to himself than to me.

"Go, then," I said. "I'm fine."

He took his phone out of his pocket and stared at it, in the way people often stare at their phones, looking for an answer without knowing what the question is, except that Ethan's phone appeared to be asleep, with a blank screen. For a while, he didn't move.

"I can skip it," he said. "Just let me message them."

"It's fine. Don't worry."

"No—it's not fine. I'll walk home with you."

"You don't have to. Go to your band practice."

"Shut up," he said. "I'm coming with you."

Of all the many hundreds of times Ethan had told me to shut up in the course of my life, this was the kindest.

A new me, hopefully with balls

The three of us set off for home, walking side by side, with an odd silence hanging in the air. We couldn't pretend my almost-fight with Felipe hadn't just happened, but none of us seemed to know what to say about it.

Eventually, Ethan broke the awkwardness by asking if I was okay.

"Yeah, I'm fine. Totally fine," I answered, though, to be honest, my adrenaline-fuelled euphoria now seemed to be wearing off, leaving me slightly wobbly and emotional.

I don't like feeling emotional. The onset of emotions makes me feel tense, and I dislike feeling tense even more than I dislike feeling emotional.

"I think I could have had him," I said, aiming for the kind of gung ho cheerfulness I wanted to be feeling. "Don't you think?"

"You and *him?*" chirped Freya. "He would have ground you to a pulp! You'd be burger meat right now if I hadn't saved you."

"He's big but he's soft," I said.

"And you're skinny and soft," she replied.

"How come you're suddenly the expert on street fighting?"

"Pressure points is what you need," she said, oblivious to my sarcasm. "If you touch someone in the right place you can paralyze them with one finger. My friend Hannah's big brother told me, but he wouldn't show me where the place is in case he paralyzed me by accident."

"Listen!" said Ethan. "Fighting's not the answer. You need to do something about this."

"About what?" I asked.

"How long has he been bullying you?"

"It wasn't really bullying."

"A guy twice your size picking a fight is bullying."

"He isn't twice my size! I'm not a dwarf. And how do you know it was him that picked the fight?"

"Because you're an idiot, but you're not that much of an idiot. It's bullying. We should report it."

"No. I don't want to."

"Has he done it before?"

"No."

"Does he pick on you?"

"No. Not usually. Anyway, it's not him in particular. It's everyone. They just ignore me. Everyone ignores me. If I make a fuss about what happened it will only make everything worse."

"It might not."

"It will. And don't tell Mom. She'll go completely over-the-top about the whole thing. I can handle that guy. He's nothing."

We walked a little farther, Ethan brooding quietly by my side.

"So why is it you they're after?" he asked.

I shrugged and gave a squashed Coke can on the pavement a kick, sending it skittering into the gutter.

"You have no idea?" said Ethan.

"No."

"You ever think maybe you're setting yourself up as a victim?"

"I'm not doing *anything*!"

"Exactly."

"What do you mean?"

"You're not doing anything to fit in."

"Like what? What are you talking about?"

"Well, look at yourself."

"What about me?"

"Can't you see it?"

"See what?"

"Does anyone else at school wear cheapo baggy old jeans, a Gap sweatshirt, and mud-stained white sneakers?"

"What, you think this is about clothes?"

"No, it's about attitude."

"What are you talking about?"

"You've got to try harder. To not be so uncool."

"This is who I am. It's always been fine. Why should I have to change just because I've been sent to some pretentious artsy-fartsy school?"

"Because that pretentious artsy-fartsy school is where you're going to have to go every week for the next three years. And if you don't change to fit the school, you're going to be miserable. You have to stop being so . . . normal."

"But I am normal. I like being normal."

"Well, you can be normal and miserable, or you can step up and fit in and enjoy yourself. It's that simple."

"And how am I going to do that?"

"Just put it on. Think of something. Find a way to be different."

"Like what?"

Ethan gazed skyward for a few seconds, deep in thought, his pace slowing to a shuffle. He then looked at me, put a hand on my shoulder, and said, "You want to know a secret?"

"What?"

He turned his head to check on Freya, who had now fallen behind us and was busily narrating to herself a story that seemed to revolve around a hilltop unicorn sanctuary of some kind being besieged by a group of lions led by a small child who either was or wasn't a real prince, depending on whether you believed the lions or the unicorns. In other words, though she was within earshot, she was entirely distracted and had no interest in anything Ethan or I were saying.

"You can't tell *anyone*," said Ethan.

"Okay."

"The thing is, I'm not actually gay."

"What?"

"I'm not gay."

"So why did you say you are?"

"I'm not definitely not."

"What?"

"I mean, I *could* be. If I put my mind to it."

"Put your mind to it?"

"I can be whatever I want. I don't need to be defined. It's just words."

"You've totally lost me. Are you gay or straight?"

"I don't buy into those binary definitions any more. It's archaic."

"Do you like girls or boys?"

"Girls. Basically. At the moment."

"So why did you come out as gay?"

"It's a queer band. You have to have a *thing*. You have to be different."

"I'm still really confused."

"Strictly speaking, it's an LGBTQ band, and I'm more at the B or maybe the Q end of things, though between you and me it's only the straight half of the B that I'm actually interested in pursuing at the moment."

"I have literally no idea what you're talking about."

"Listen—a band needs an angle. An edge. And you know what I've realized? It's the craziest discovery."

"What?"

"Being gay is the most *amazing* way to get girls. It's incredible."

"Hang on, hang on. To get *girls*?"

"Yeah."

"That doesn't make any sense!"

"I know. But it works."

"How?"

"I swear, it's incredible. Now that I'm gay, girls love me. They're all over me. Hugging, gossiping, inviting me to their homes, up into their bedrooms, it's like magic."

"Yeah, but . . . if they think you're gay . . ."

"Bi-curious."

"What does that even mean?"

"It means whatever you want it to mean! That's what's so great!"

"Isn't this whole thing a bit . . . twisted?"

"Look—I was a total friendless freak in Stevenage. For years. Like you are now. No offense. And now, for the first time in my life, I'm popular. I'm *cool*! It's the best thing that's ever happened to me."

"Are you saying I should be gay?"

"NO! We can't both do it."

"What then?"

"I don't know. You've just got to stop being so aloof from everything."

"How did you know I was being aloof? I didn't think anyone had noticed."

"Maybe aloof's the wrong word. It's not like you act superior. What you're doing is behaving as if you think you're inferior."

"That's not coming from me! Everyone looks down on me like I'm some kind of weirdo loser. And I'm not! At least, I never was before."

"If you behave as if you hate everyone, everyone's going to hate you."

"You're saying everyone actually hates me?"

"I'm saying you have to find a way to join in."

"With what?"

"Something. Anything. That's what you've got to figure out."

Though I was totally baffled by his sexuality gambit, I could see he had a point about this. If I stayed as I was, I'd never get used to that school, and the school would never accept me.

There was, as yet, no plan of action, but the notion that I had a choice—that I could alter my own behavior to improve my situation—was a new and hopeful one. Mom had already told me the exact same thing, repeatedly, but that didn't count. This time it actually sank in.

I had no idea what specifically to change, but somewhere deep inside me I felt the beginnings of an inkling that something might come up. I knew I couldn't transform myself overnight, but I also felt that just looking at the world with eyes that were seeking an opportunity for change, rather than approaching each school day with defeatist dread, was in itself a step forward. I had stood up to Felipe, after all. That, perhaps, could be my turning point.

The Sam I used to be, in Stevenage, was no use in this new world. The only way to find a place for myself here was to somehow build a new me. If I continued on as I was,

Felipe and his kind would crush me. I had no choice but to reinvent myself and fight back.

Spotting another soda can a few steps ahead of us on the pavement, I accelerated to give it a kick, but Ethan sped up too, barging into me with his shoulder. At the last second I pushed him off the pavement and got to the can first.

"Cheat," he said, smiling, as we turned the corner onto our road.

"So how are you going to break it to Mom?" I asked.

"What?"

"That you're straight."

"I don't know," said Ethan. "She's going to be heart-broken. I'm not sure I can tell her."

"You'll have to at some point."

"It's too awkward."

"What about girlfriends?"

"Gay men can have girlfriends."

"Not that kind of girlfriend."

"She'll figure it out eventually. Listen, you have to promise you won't say anything. To anyone. If you do, I'll cut your nuts off."

"It won't make any difference," I said. "I don't think a girl has ever looked at me with any interest ever. Not once. In fifteen years."

"Well, that's why you have to *do* something with yourself. You can't just sit and wait for life to happen to you. You have to go out and grab it."

"Mmm."

"Life, that is. Not girls. You can't just grab girls."

"I know. I know. I'm not Donald Trump."

"And if those drama assholes come after you again, you tell me. Okay?"

"Okay."

"Don't let anyone push you around. Ever. Except me."

I gave him a shove, took out my key, and opened the front door.

Mom immediately appeared in the hall, wearing an apron, holding a jar of lurid purple gloop—at first glance either homemade jam or radioactive waste. Both possibilities were equally out of character. This was clearly something to do with her blog.

"Hello, darlings," she chirped. "Did you all have a stimulating day?"

A moment of brotherly genius

It turned out Mom was not, after all, writing a blog about do-it-yourself nuclear reprocessing. The stuff in the jar was, apparently, jam and was supposedly edible.

A complicated explanation of something to do with jam and the link between creativity and seasonal eating filled the kitchen like hippie white noise as we gathered for the evening meal. Dad's only question, as he shoved piles of empty Whole Foods blackberry containers into the recycling, was to ask if the homemade jam, which took her all afternoon to make, was cheaper than jam you could buy ready-made.

"That's completely missing the point," replied Mom.

"There's a point?" asked Ethan.

Mom let out a my-family-doesn't-appreciate-me sigh.

While Ethan and Dad exchanged a guilty glance, Freya,

who was finely attuned to Mom's moods, said, "I think it looks lovely."

"Thank you, darling," said Mom, kissing her on the forehead.

"Is it paint?" asked Freya, smiling guilelessly.

"Um . . . no, dear. It's jam. As I've been explaining for the last ten minutes."

"Jam? You're supposed to *eat* it?"

Mom took three deep breaths.

"What are we going to do with all that jam?" continued Freya. "That's enough for about five years!"

"Let's all sit down and have dinner, shall we?" said Mom. "How was school today?"

We took our places as Mom served up an alarmingly zucchini-heavy vegetable slop. The glory days of the junk-food Love Bomb era were definitively over. As if to make this doubly clear, Mom had even made brown rice.

"Freya?" said Mom.

"Yes?" she replied, gazing dismally at her heavily loaded plate.

"How was school?"

"Good."

"Did anything happen?"

"No."

"Nothing at all?"

131

"No."

"Tell me one thing."

Freya looked up from her food, sighed, and said, "Well, we did the planets and I made Saturn out of some untwisted coat hangers and mush and cut-up paper plates and Miss Watson said it was exceptional and at lunchtime Jonah pushed Zac off a wall and he had to go away in an ambulance so Jonah was sent to the principal and after he came back he just sat and wouldn't speak then he got some scissors and scratched something into his desk so Miss Watson sent him out into the corridor and when he was out there he spat on the window so he got sent to the principal again then at final bell we waited forever and ever for Sam because Ethan had band practice and he didn't come and Ethan used all the words I'm not allowed to say including the one beginning with *F* that's about how a man and a woman make babies then he sent me to find him and when I did he was being bullied by a really big guy and they were about to have a fight but I went in and saved him and then Ethan said he didn't have to go to band practice after all and we walked home."

Mom and Dad stared aghast at Freya, who was now lifting two grains of rice warily toward her mouth.

"Is this true?" said Mom, turning her attention to Ethan and me.

"No!" I said.

"Are you being bullied?" asked Dad.

"No! Of course not!"

"If you are, we have to tell the school. We have to do something about it," said Mom.

"I'm fine! He's a friend from my class and we were messing around. Freya's confused."

"No I'm not! I saw the whole thing," said Freya. "And on the way home they talked about girls and Ethan told Sam a secret about something to do with LTBQ, which I think is a secret code."

One of the strange things about Freya is that even though she never gives the impression of listening, it sometimes turns out that she is. Even when apparently totally absorbed in her own fantasy world, she occasionally turns around and reveals that she knows exactly what's been going on.

Ethan and I shot a glance at each other. We had to stop Freya from talking, immediately.

"I heard him say that to crack the code you have to cut the B in half," she continued, "which is a big clue, but I haven't figured out how . . ."

"I think you should tell them," interrupted Ethan, jabbing a fork in my direction.

"Tell them *what?*" I said through clenched teeth. Was he selling me down the river to preserve his own secret?

"Sam's ... um ... what he's done is ... without telling anyone, he's ... joined a drama group," said Ethan. "He's being all embarrassed about it, for some reason, so he never even told me, which is why I got confused over who was supposed to be walking Freya home. He and this guy were doing an improvisation, trying to see how convincing they could be, and everyone fell for it and thought it was a real fight. It was brilliant. Freya went nuts."

Genius! My brother, when he wasn't being an epic pain in the rear end, was a genius.

"Yeah," I added. "It's true. The auditions for the school play are next week, and there's a group that are doing some workshops beforehand. You know. As preparation."

"But half the school was right there in a big circle shouting at them to fight!" said Freya. "It was real!"

"That was the whole point," I said firmly. "She's confused."

Freya's wily little seven-year-old eyes peered at me, and her mouth clenched into a resentful pout. She had an annoying habit of becoming suddenly and uncharacteristically rigid about matters of fact versus fiction at the most inconvenient moments. I returned her look with a keep-it-zipped stare, which she seemed to understand.

"You've joined a drama group?" said Mom, using the tone of voice a normal parent might reserve for the moment you inform them you've won a Nobel Prize.

"Yeah," I said, with a pseudo-shy shrug.

"After school? With friends?"

"It's just a bit of improvising."

"Oh, that's wonderful. That is fantastic news. I'm *so* pleased."

"Are you sure you're okay?" said Dad. "Nobody's picking on you?"

"It was acting!" said Mom. "Weren't you listening? He's taking part in things! He's joined a drama club!"

"I heard. I was just checking."

"Listen," said Mom, turning back to me. "You know my friend Francine? From the school fundraising committee? She was here the other day."

"Francine? Which one's that? Is she the one with . . . um . . . long hair?" I said, grasping at any topic of conversation that wasn't bullying.

"Yes. Huge brown eyes. Expensive jewelry. Beautiful deep voice."

"Um . . ."

"Anyway, she's a professional actress and she says her daughter is *really* talented, and she's in your year. Have you come across a girl named Jennifer?"

My undercarriage gave an immediate involuntary twitch, like a phone announcing a notification.

"That's her mom? Jennifer's in my class."

"So you're already friends?"

"Well . . . kind of. In a way."

"Because if you're hoping to get into the school play, she's someone you should talk to. Francine was telling me how Jennifer's one of the best actors in the school. I was about to say we could invite them over so you could get to know her better, but if you're friends already . . ."

"No! Yes! I mean, I don't know her that well. Hardly at all, really, so that would be good."

"Only if you feel like it."

"Well . . . you know . . . why not? Might as well. Can't do any harm. Can it? So . . . might as well. Just . . . you know . . . whenever . . . no big deal."

"Okay. I'll text Francine."

Just the idea of Jennifer's visit set my pulse throbbing. Was this the worst or the best idea I had ever heard?

I wasn't sure.

Did I want that gorgeous, intimidating, wonderful, vain girl in my house? Did I want to have to talk to her?

Of course I did! Of course I didn't! Of course I did! Etc.

Whether I wanted it or not (Of course I did! Of course I didn't!), events were now in motion. Jennifer, at some point in the near future, would appear in my house. Where I lived.

Jennifer!

In my house.

Actually genuinely visiting, in person.

Physically entering the rooms inhabited by my family.

From the moment Mom confirmed the visit, this prospect filled my every waking hour with a mixture of nervous dread and underpant-stirring overexcitement. This might sound like a perfectly normal state of mind for a boy of my age—and I suppose it was—but anticipating Jennifer's arrival in my home made it infinitely worse.

The sulky angel and her confiscated phone

While I struggled to find anyone I liked at school, despite being stuck there five days a week, Mom had somehow embedded herself into the school-mom network right away, and from the first week seemed to know and love everyone even vaguely connected to the North London Academy for the Gifted and Talented.

These new friends constantly appeared in our house, roosting noisily around our kitchen table clutching mugs of coffee. There was Gabriella, an "internet entrepreneur" who imported fair-trade ponchos from a women's collective in rural Mexico. There was Adrienne, a "homemaker" who was considering retraining as a shaman, though whether or not this had anything to do with her son being universally known as a drug dealer was unclear. There was Lala (yes, really), an insanely beautiful part-time yoga teacher, who had a voice like maple syrup, seemed to wear Lycra in all weather, and made my dad so nervous he couldn't speak. And there was Francine, the actor, Jennifer's mother.

Francine was *very* actory. When she spoke, whatever she was saying, she made it sound like a profound and terrible confession. If you asked her how she was, she'd answer, "I'm fine, but I got stuck in terrible traffic on Finchley Road," using the heavy, tragic intonation of someone announcing that their son was missing in action at Dunkirk. She only ever wore mauve and black, and was always so shrouded in complex drapes of fabric that when she reached for her coffee you never knew where a limb might appear.

When I arrived home from school to find Francine at the kitchen table opposite Mom, my heart immediately began to palpitate with Jennifer-fear. Was she also in the house? Was this The Visit? I couldn't relax until I knew. When I did know, I still wouldn't be able to relax, especially if she was here, but I had to have the information as quickly as possible, so as to arrange my tension levels to an appropriate setting. A bit like if you found yourself in a room with someone holding a hand grenade. You'd want to know if the pin was in or out.

"Sam, darling," intoned Francine. "How *are* you?"

She made her question sound as if she wasn't merely asking if I'd had a good day but wanted an insight into every detail of my inner well-being. Her tone of voice also seemed to imply that my answer was something on which her very future depended.

"Fine," I said. "Can I have a cookie?"

"Oh, take, take," said Francine, holding out a plateful of the Fancy Cookies Mom Bought for Guests. "You'll be doing me a favor."

Mom flicked me her don't-eat-them-all eyes.

"Now, your mother tells me you've joined a drama group. That's *wonderful* news. You have an everyman quality that I feel could take you a long way."

"Well, it's only a . . ."

"Jennifer tells me nothing. Nothing," said Francine, turning back to face Mom. "She's in a terribly conflictual phase. Of course, it's what you expect at this age, but the moods! Honestly! *Quelle horreur!*"

"Is she here?" I asked, as casually as I could manage. I followed the question up with a short cough, in the hope this might add to the impression of haughty indifference, though I think it may have had the opposite effect.

"Physically, yes; mentally, no," said Francine, waving a hand in the direction of the living room. "She's off in cyberspace, as usual, doing God knows what with God knows who. Honestly, this phone thing is just appalling, isn't it? The obsession!"

"Oh, it drives me nuts," said Mom. "It's a constant battle."

On and on they droned, through the endlessly repeated everything-was-so-much-better-in-ye-olden-days-before-the-internet-came-along-and-ruined-all-our-lives-by-making-everything-easier conversation that seems to hold some kind of infinite fascination for people over the age of forty, while my mind drifted off into a frantic internal debate:

Me: Go and talk to Jennifer!
Me: I will. In a minute.
Me: No—now.
Me: In a second. When I'm ready.
Me: What are you waiting for?
Me: I'm not ready.
Me: You'd rather sit in the kitchen with your mom than talk to the girl you've been fantasizing about for weeks on end? What's wrong with you?
Me: I'm just not ready yet.
Me: What are you afraid of?
Me: Nothing.
Me: You are! You're afraid!
Me: Okay! I'm afraid!
Me: Of what?
Me: Everything! Humiliation! Rejection! Failure! And every female on the planet older than thirteen!
Me: Well, don't be! Man up!

It was at this point that I realized I had absentmindedly eaten almost all the cookies. I only noticed this was happening when I saw my hand reaching for the last one.

I swiftly moved the almost-empty plate out of Mom's eyeline.

Clearly, it was time to step up and take action. A dual-pronged plan began to take shape. In one stroke, by offering this final cookie to Jennifer, I could dispose of all incriminating snack-consumption evidence and give myself a conversational opening. One of the hardest things with Jennifer was knowing what to say to her, and "Would you like a cookie?" was a slam dunk.

I stood up.

I lifted the plate containing the solitary cookie.

Tamping down all fear and self-doubt, I set off in search of Jennifer, and soon found her curled up on the sofa in a shaft of early-evening sunlight, swiping at her phone.

"Hi," I said. "D'you want a cookie?"

"Naa," she replied, without looking up.

For this to turn into a conversation I now needed to say something else. After racking my brains to come up with an interesting topic or witty line, I eventually said, "Sure?"

She shrugged.

My slam-dunk opening hadn't exactly come off. We seemed to have run aground faster than I'd hoped.

I stood there for a while, watching her ignore me, then walked back to the kitchen, eating the final cookie.

Oh, yes. Casanova had nothing on me. Pure charisma.

"Back already?" said Francine. "Did she ignore you?"

"No, she just didn't want any . . . er, I mean, I gave her a few cookies. Several, in fact. That's why there's none left."

"She won't eat them," said Francine.

My cookie story was crumbling. So to speak.

"If you want her attention, you have to text her. Or WhatsApp her. Or Snapchat. Or whatever it is you people are doing these days. Honestly, even if you're in the same room it's the only way to get her to notice you exist."

"I don't have her number," I said.

"I wasn't being serious. But let's try it. Give me your phone." I handed it over. Francine typed in a number and handed it back to me. "Offer her a coffee. She always wants more coffee."

I typed the message. A second later, my phone pinged. Francine and Mom laughed.

"See?" said Francine triumphantly. "She wants another coffee. Am I right?"

I looked at the screen.

"No."

"No? What does she say?"

"She says, 'Where did you get my number?'"

"Aggghh! That girl!"

Francine stood and marched from the room. Sounds of a muffled argument became audible through the wall, during which Mom and I couldn't look at each other; then Francine and Jennifer returned together. Francine was holding Jennifer's phone.

"Jennifer's going to join us for a coffee!" said Francine in a voice so frantically cheerful it was practically psychotic. "She's going to make conversation."

Jennifer was wearing the facial expression of someone who has bitten into a raw onion.

"So . . . Jennifer . . . your mother tells me you're a very talented actress," said Mom.

"Actor," said Jennifer.

"Don't be rude," said Francine.

"You told me actress was sexist!" said Jennifer.

"Anyway," said Mom. "Are you in this same drama group as Sam?"

Jennifer looked up, making eye contact with my mother for the first time. "Sam's in an acting group?"

"Yes, they had their first rehearsal last week."

Jennifer turned her head and stared suspiciously at me. I felt my insides shrivel.

"I . . . I never said it was an acting *group*," I stammered. "It's just an improvisation thing."

"How *wonderful!*" said Francine. "I simply *adore* the

freedom of improvisation. It's like shedding a skin. You just *become* the character. Don't you find?"

"Kind of," I said. "Anyway, Finchley Road, eh. The traffic's just awful, isn't it?"

"What did you improvise?" asked Francine.

"Um . . ." I was on the brink of making another attempt to change the subject when a strange revelation swept through me. Jennifer was beautiful to look at, but she was also rude and arrogant, and she was part of the gang that really had been bullying me. I'd kept the incident quiet and helped her friend get away with it, but why, when she couldn't be bothered to look at me or grunt more than a single syllable when I tried to start a conversation, was I continuing to go out of my way to make this easy for her?

I had stood up to Felipe. Perhaps I had to stand up to Jennifer too.

"It was a fight scene," I said. "Jennifer was there. She'll tell you."

Her cheeks flushed, and she miraculously managed to look even more pissed off than her previous onion-face. "Oh, it was a . . . kind of . . . verbal-sparring type thing," she said. "Just messing around."

"It was in the playground, apparently," said Mom. "After school. Freya saw it and she was so convinced she thought they were actually bullying him. Isn't that funny?"

"Was Felipe there?" asked Francine, staring at Jennifer, her voice tight and suspicious.

Jennifer looked down at her hands and shrugged.

"There was an incident last year," said Francine, turning to Mom, "involving a boy who was withdrawn from the school. A very unhappy boy. Felipe and a couple of his friends were suspended for bullying." She turned to me and, speaking with even more intensity than she gave to her descriptions of bad traffic, said, "Was Felipe involved in this?"

"Um . . . kind of," I said, glancing toward Jennifer, who was now looking at me with big, pleading, sexy eyes. Not that she was *doing* sexy eyes. She just had sexy eyes. She had sexy everything. I couldn't even look at her fingernails without thinking inappropriate thoughts. And I certainly couldn't look at her big, pleading, sexy eyes while sustaining a desire for revenge. "But . . . it wasn't like that. I wasn't . . . like . . . I mean . . ."

"You enjoyed it," suggested Jennifer.

A thick silence filled the room. The moment was delicately poised. Glancing again at Jennifer, I decided that although I did get some pleasure from making her squirm and showing her that I wasn't a complete pushover, I didn't want her to hate me.

"Yeah," I said. "It was fun."

"Sam was excellent. He's talented. We were all really

impressed," added Jennifer, in a voice that, if she was as good an actor as everyone seemed to think, probably wouldn't have sounded so obviously relieved.

I looked across at the two moms, both of whom were staring at us in the way shop security guards stare at loitering teenagers.

"You enjoyed it?" asked Mom, with heavy emphasis.

"Yeah. It was good."

"There was no bullying?" asked Francine.

"No!" said Jennifer.

"No," I added. "It was fine. Good, actually. Lots of really . . . deep . . ."

"Emotions?" said Jennifer.

"Yeah. Emotions. And stuff like that. They all said I should audition for the school play."

"Oh, you must!" said Francine, lurching forward and clutching my forearm. "You must, you simply must! Every year it's an *event*. There's no other word for it. Mr. Duverne is a miracle worker."

"I might," I said cagily.

"Perhaps the two of you could work on an audition piece together," said Francine pointedly, with an edge to her voice that implied she didn't fully believe her daughter's improvisation/bullying cover-up.

"Well . . . I've got lots of other friends I usually rehearse with"—Jennifer seemed to wither slightly under her mother's stare—"but that might be good. Yeah."

"Great!" said Francine. "It's so important to be welcoming to the new faces in the class. Sam's got your number now, so he can text you when he's ready."

"Yeah," said Jennifer. "I suppose. If you don't have anyone else."

"You'd like that wouldn't you, Jennifer?" said Francine.

"Yes! I already said! Can I have my phone back now?"

"When we've said our goodbyes. Don't be rude."

As soon as they left, I could tell that Mom wanted to quiz me further about bullying, so I pleaded urgent homework and ran straight upstairs.

I sat down at my desk and discovered, to my surprise, that I actually did have urgent homework to finish, but there was no way that was going to happen. My mind was racing with a frantic internal debate about what I should do next:

OPTIMISTIC BRAIN: We have to audition for the school play. This is exactly what Ethan said we should do.

PESSIMISTIC BRAIN: You're only saying that to get closer to Jennifer, even though you know she's a snobby, self-important princess who thinks you're a total geek. We should stay away from her.

DICK: *Rubbish. She's gorgeous. Don't be a loser. Rehearse with her.*

OPTIMISTIC BRAIN: *Yes, this is a great chance to find our place in the school.*

PESSIMISTIC BRAIN: *The school play will be filled with people like Felipe. Everyone we hate.*

DICK: *And Jennifer! She's gorgeous.*

PESSIMISTIC BRAIN: *Jennifer has zero interest in us, and she's also selfish and pretentious.*

DICK: *And gorgeous.*

PESSIMISTIC BRAIN: *Why's that so important?*

DICK: *She's just gorgeous.*

PESSIMISTIC BRAIN: *Will you stop saying that?*

DICK: *She's gorgeous.*

OPTIMISTIC BRAIN: *Listen, you guys. This isn't all about Jennifer. We need to work together and do something—like Ethan said—to make friends and fit in. Otherwise school is just going to be hell this year and next year and the year after.*

PESSIMISTIC BRAIN: *Why on earth would we volunteer to spend lots of extra time at school, with people we don't even like?*

DICK: *Because some of them are female and gorgeous.*

OPTIMISTIC BRAIN: *Because making some extra effort is the only way to turn this around.*

PESSIMISTIC BRAIN: They hate us. They think we're boring.

OPTIMISTIC BRAIN: Well, if we join in and take part in something creative, and show them that we're not just someone who hangs around at the edge of everything looking miserable, then maybe they'll see another side to us and stop hating us.

DICK: We've got her phone number. We've got an excuse to text her. End of story.

PESSIMISTIC BRAIN: Only geriatrics send text messages.

DICK: SHUT IT!

PESSIMISTIC BRAIN: Don't talk to me like that.

DICK: I'll talk to you however I want.

PESSIMISTIC BRAIN: Why should I be pushed around by you?

DICK: Because I'm in charge.

PESSIMISTIC BRAIN: Says who?

DICK: ME! You'll get your turn when we're fifty or something, but for now I'm the boss, so shut your mouth, stop whimpering, and do your homework.

PESSIMISTIC AND OPTIMISTIC BRAIN: Why do we have to do all the homework?

DICK: Why d'you think? Now stop whining and get on with it, you losers. I need a nap. And my naps only last about ten minutes, so you'd better get moving.

Modern romance

Hi Jennifer. Sam here. Auditions for the school play are coming up and we were talking about maybe getting together to rehearse something beforehand so I was wondering if you'd like to meet up some time? ☺

No

Picking insects out of Felipe's hair

A week after this touching exchange of love notes I found myself in the drama room, sitting in a large circle, saying "oooooooooooooh" for five minutes, scooping "from the bottom to the top of my vocal range, focusing on the sensation of reverberations in my head and neck, exploring the sound, trying to *be* the syllable." No, I hadn't been committed to an insane asylum. This was my audition for *The Tempest*.

Exactly how the ability to say "oooooooooooooh" revealed your skill at reciting Elizabethan dialogue was a mystery, but Mr. Duverne had his methods, which were not to be questioned.

Even with my extremely limited knowledge of Shakespeare, I would have gladly bet every penny I owned on *The Tempest* not containing a scene where thirty teenagers sat in a circle and went "oooooooooooooooooooh" until someone fainted from hyperventilation.

The next stage of the audition was another "warm-up exercise" called "mystery carry," in which you had to walk across the room carrying a mimed object, using your body to "reveal the essence—the weight, shape, and form" of what you were carrying.

Felipe went first and did an elaborate mime involving much grimacing, pouting, and bicep flexing, which nobody guessed. With a pseudo-modest shrug and a knowing smirk, he eventually revealed that his object was a live python, which I suspect was an oblique reference to his sexual prowess.

Several more animals followed, then Jennifer went up and did another unfathomable routine, which it turned out was her attempt at "an old crone carrying firewood through the forest." Mr. Duverne told her this was excellent, even though the only guesses had been "Something heavy" and "Are you a wounded dolphin?"

When I was called up, I opted for something simple and mimed carrying a plate of food. When Mr. Duverne asked me what kind of food, I said I didn't know. He told me he could see in my eyes that I didn't know, which is why the mime wasn't working, and said I should try again. I walked across the stage once more, thinking to myself, "Burger

burger burger burger", but I don't think this made for a huge improvement.

When I sat back down, Felipe leaned toward me and whispered in my ear, "Did you not realize that when I said you should audition, I was giving you shit?"

I opened my mouth to floor him with a cutting and witty response, but unfortunately my brain failed to supply one.

"I can't believe you actually came," he added, before sliding back into his chair and muttering something into Jennifer's ear.

I was rapidly reaching the conclusion that despite my sincere intention to turn my life around by joining in the cultural life of the school, this whole drama thing just wasn't for me. If I'd been able to think of an excuse I probably would have left, but it somehow didn't feel possible to walk out in the middle, even though, for the first time since arriving at the school, I'd found myself staying late for an after-school club.

The words "What were you thinking?" went around and around my head on a deafening loop for the remainder of the audition, which seemed to consist almost entirely of what I would have called children's party games, though Mr. Duverne conducted proceedings with the seriousness of a scientist monitoring a team of lab technicians (even though those lab technicians might, at any given moment, be acting out the life cycle of an acorn).

By the time we got to the final exercise/game/ humiliating waste of time, I was desperate to get home. The last task was to improvise a character in front of the group, which another person would have to mirror in real time.

As usual, Felipe volunteered to go first. To my horror, Mr. Duverne nominated me to be his partner. Felipe looked even more unhappy about this than I did.

He took the lead and mimed a man getting out of bed, shaving, and putting on a suit. I copied him to the best of my abilities—as in, not very well at all.

When Mr. Duverne said it was time to switch roles, a crazy idea popped into my mind. Out of the blue, a feeling of liberating indifference descended on me. I knew I didn't want to be in this play—even if it was a chance to get closer to Jennifer—and I also felt that I suddenly didn't care what these people thought of me. If a whole group has decided you are insignificant and boring, you can't really embarrass yourself in front of them, because their opinion of you can't go any lower. Which meant this game opened up an opportunity for a delicious revenge on Felipe. Here I was, stuck on an audition stage with the vainest boy in the world, and his task, if he wanted to prove he was as great an actor as he considered himself to be, was to copy everything I did for the next five minutes.

These two things put together struck me as a golden ticket. I no longer cared about making myself look stupid, and the opportunity to make Felipe look stupid had landed in my lap.

I tucked my hands under my armpits, stuck my lips out, and began to grunt like a monkey. The look of dismay on Felipe's face was beautiful.

Half-heartedly, he began to copy me.

I danced in place, grunting more excitedly, then began to pick fleas out of my fur and eat them.

Felipe, to my absolute delight, looked like he wanted to kill me. I yapped angrily at him, in what was unmistakeably monkey language for "What are you waiting for, you dunce?"

Reluctantly, he stepped up his monkey efforts. Most of the audience was now laughing. Out of the corner of my eye I could see that Jennifer was one of them.

I hopped up close to Felipe and stared at him. He stared back, his eyes brimming with rage and confusion.

I began to groom him, messing up his complicatedly gelled hair, then started picking imaginary insects off his head and putting them in my mouth.

When I offered him a taste of a half-chewed parasite, he

slapped my hand away and said, "Don't touch me, you freak!"

This got a big laugh, and a thrilling realization hit me. Everyone in the room (except perhaps Mr. Duverne) knew what was going on. I clearly wasn't the only one who had been belittled, mocked, or intimidated by Felipe, and this audience was now on my side, not his. The more uncomfortable I could make him, the more everyone would laugh. Up here, onstage, I could be as ridiculous as possible, but whatever I did, the joke wouldn't be on me; it would be on him.

I yapped and jumped more angrily than ever, summoning up the monkey body language for "This thing here isn't a monkey! He's a human and an impostor!"

Felipe had by now given up on copying me. He tried to walk offstage, but I stepped up my angry-monkey routine and blocked his exit.

"This isn't funny," he said.

I scratched my ass and wafted my fingers toward his face.

He pushed me away, so I ran behind him, jumped on his back, and began to yelp in his ear at the top of my voice. He staggered around the stage, trying to shake me off, but I clung on as hard as I could. Now even Mr. Duverne was laughing.

"Get off me, you prick!" yelled Felipe.

I grunted and huffed loudly and rhythmically, like a monkey whose thoughts are beginning to turn from aggression to love.

The whole room was now in hysterics.

Mr. Duverne stood up and, projecting impressively over the hoots of laughter, said, "Okay, guys! Great work. That's enough, thanks."

I jumped down from Felipe's back and, with the sound of applause ringing in my ears, took a bow.

This was, by a considerable margin, the happiest moment I'd ever had at this school. Possibly the only happy moment, to be honest. It didn't occur to me that Mr. Duverne would count my attempt to humiliate Felipe as acting, but while the group was filing out, he took me aside, congratulated me on my "committed work" and said, "I've seen new potential in you."

This was the kind of hollow praise teachers spouted all the time, but he went on to add that I stood a strong chance of getting called back for the second round of auditions. "I need a good Caliban," he said.

"What's that?"

"He's a significant character. Part man, part beast. I want someone who can portray hidden depths of anger and resentment, concealed behind a servile, lonely, and tragic exterior. I think you may have the capacity for that."

"Thanks," I said. This was, at best, a distinctly back-handed compliment.

"There are also some moments of comedy, which you might have a talent for. Take a look at the text."

"Okay. I will," I lied.

Feeling more confused than ever, I walked home. In the final minutes of that audition something strange had taken place. My certainty that I didn't want to be in the play had released me to do something that had made Mr. Duverne want me for it. Did that mean I now ought to change my mind back again? Should I be so easily swayed by this tiny compliment? Or was it not Mr. Duverne but the response of the audience that was making me reconsider? That moment, jumping onto Felipe's back and sending the whole group into waves of laughter, had been intoxicating. I'd been acting like a total idiot, messing around as much as the wildest toddler, yet I felt in absolute control, not just of myself but of the whole room. This was a sensation of extraordinary power that I'd never felt before.

I knew it was wrong to want to do something just because you felt flattered to be asked, but as I approached home, mulling over the possibility of getting cast in the school play, I realized I wanted the feeling of performing to an audience again. There was something amazing about being onstage, about being yourself but not yourself, licensed to go crazy in the name of entertaining an audience. Making people laugh was a thrilling buzz. I spent all my time at school feeling utterly invisible, and what I'd done in that audition felt like the opposite of invisibility.

As I slotted my key into the front door, I knew I had changed my mind. This was no longer just about getting closer to Jennifer. I wanted to be chosen for the man-beast. Even if it meant spending hours of my life doing idiotic drama games, even if it meant I'd be stuck in long rehearsals with some of the most pretentious people I'd ever met, I wanted that part.

Marshmallow palace flying high

By the time I had actually opened the door and walked inside, I wasn't so sure. Being home made me contemplate the idea of actually telling someone that I was hoping to go up onstage and act, and the idea of admitting this made me feel queasy. If I was scared of simply *telling* someone I might be taking up acting, what chance did I have of being brave enough to stand on a stage in front of hundreds of strangers actually doing it?

This in turn made me wonder if other people doubted every decision they made the minute they made it, or if that was just me. Which made me wonder if it was paranoid to wonder if the weird things about yourself were unique. Which made me wonder if it was normal to feel paranoid about completely normal trains of thought. If they were normal. Which maybe they weren't. By which point I completely lost track of what I was worrying about. Which was a relief. Except also not, because I still felt worried. Though whether I was worrying about one of the things I was worried about or was now just worrying about the fact that I felt worried was anyone's guess.

This soothing and productive train of thought was interrupted by a sudden blast of noise from upstairs. It sounded as if a team of road workers had installed themselves in Ethan's bedroom and begun to jackhammer some pavement. The noise then got louder, which made me think it probably wasn't mere industrial-scale destruction but was in fact some kind of pan-galactic apocalypse. Then I remembered this was the day of Ethan's band rehearsal. They'd rehearsed a few times at other people's houses; now it was our turn.

I looked out of the kitchen window and saw that Mom was in her studio at the bottom of the garden. Wearing noise-canceling handphones.

If I didn't want to hear the noise I needed to leave the house or, rather, the street. In fact, I'd probably have to travel a couple of stops on the Underground. This wasn't really practical, so the next best option seemed to be to go up and see for myself how a group of teenagers could make themselves sound like the end of the known universe.

I made a stop in the bathroom first to raid Mom's stock of earplugs, which she kept as a defense against Dad's snoring.

Having lumps of luminous yellow foam sticking out of my ears as I met Ethan's bandmates wasn't ideal on the hoping-to-look-cool front, but a trickle of blood oozing from my eardrums followed by decades of deafness wasn't a look I much fancied either, so I shoved in the earplugs and made my way up to Ethan's boy-cave.

I usually tiptoe the last flight of stairs up to his room in order to stop him from shouting at me to go away before I've even gotten to the door, but on this occasion I could have been playing the bagpipes and he wouldn't have heard me approach.

I was amazed to discover, on entering the room, that this mind-melting racket was being made by only four people, though three of them were plugged into coffin-size speakers, and the other one was playing a drum kit so huge it was held together with scaffolding.

Up close, the noise they made resolved itself into something almost resembling music. My brother was on lead guitar, strumming away with his instrument dangling on such a long strap it was somewhere down near his knees. On vocals and bass was the girl with short, spiky blond- and red-streaked hair who Ethan was always chatting to at the school gates. She had ice-blue eyes and was wearing gray lipstick, with a tiny stud glistening in her left nostril. She was both terrifying and terrifyingly sexy. Her singing was hard to hear over the guitar thrashing and drum whacking, but even half-drowned-out, you couldn't miss the diamond-like purity of her voice.

Darius was standing just behind the singer, looking pastier and skinnier than ever, nodding his head in time to the beat and looking completely absorbed, as if he was playing an instrument, though the only thing in front of him was a laptop. I guessed he wasn't doing his homework, though what his computer might be contributing to the music I had no idea. At second glance, a piano-keyboard type thing did seem to be connected to the laptop, which reassured me that he wasn't just standing there writing an English essay.

On drums was—a drummer. I have no idea who. The kit was so vast only the bristly top of a shaved head was visible.

Nobody seemed to notice me when I walked in, except for Freya, who was dancing happily in front of the band with a big grin on her face and her fingers in her ears. Even when the song came to a thrashy end, followed by an enthusiastic one-person round of applause from Freya, still nobody noticed I was there.

"It's not tight enough," said Darius.

"Yeah," said Ethan, though I could see by the slightly glazed look in his eyes that he didn't actually know what he was agreeing with.

"I love it!" said Freya. "It makes me feel like my head's going to explode. But why are the words so miserable?"

"I told you, if you want to stay in my room you have to be quiet," said Ethan.

"What's she doing in here, anyway?" said the almost-invisible, shaved-headed drummer, who by the sound of it was in fact female.

"She's our groupie," said Darius. "Every band needs a groupie."

"Maybe she's right," said the singer.

"What?" said Ethan. "Alt-metal psychedelia crossover is *supposed* to be miserable. That's the whole point."

"But the lyrics are all metal and no psychedelia, aren't they? They're just angry," replied the singer.

"They're supposed to be angry, but kind of a poetic slash angry slash meaningful type thing," said Ethan, using a tone of voice I'd never heard from him before. When he disagreed with me, he managed to inject every syllable with absolute confidence that I was a lower form of life whose opinions were barely worthy of sullying his eardrums. The way he spoke to the singer was the exact opposite of this.

I'm no expert in matters of the heart—in fact I know about as much about love as I do about hot-air ballooning—but even I could see Ethan was head-over-heels, hook-line-and-sinker, loop-the-loop crazy about this girl. Frankly, who could blame him?

"What if the lyrics subverted the music?" she said.

"That's a cool idea," said Darius, who was tapping away at his laptop just as intently as when the band had been playing, except that now no sound was coming out except the clicking of the keyboard. Which made me wonder if maybe he was writing an English essay after all.

"What do you mean?" said Ethan.

"What's psychedelia?" asked Freya.

"Shut up! This is a rehearsal, not a nursery," Ethan snapped.

"Psychedelia's when a song has words that are kind of crazy and don't follow the logic of ordinary life," said the singer, turning her wondrous smile toward Freya.

"What, like this?" replied Freya, passing the singer the notebook she carried around with her everywhere, which was filled with whatever pictures and stories she was working on at that particular time. "I don't normally let anyone touch my notebook, but I like your hair," she added.

"Freya—go downstairs and have some chips or something," said Ethan.

"There aren't any."

"There's a big half-eaten bag next to the toaster."

"Those aren't chips."

"Yes they are."

"They're lentil chips."

"Exactly. Chips."

"That's not chips. If it was chips it wouldn't be a half-eaten bag, it would be an empty bag, because you would have eaten them."

"This is making me hungry," said the drummer.

"Okay, forget the chips!" said Ethan. "Just . . . go and tell Mom I'm being mean to you."

"You're not being mean to me."

"Yes I am."

"No you're not."

"YES I AM! PISS OFF!"

"You only said that to try and get rid of me."

"I know! That's what 'piss off' means!"

"I think there might be something good here," said the singer, staring into Freya's notebook.

"*What?*" said Ethan, incredulous.

"It's true we could improve the chorus," said Darius. "What is it now? *I'm so lonely, lonely / Why does nobody understand me, stand me / The world is such a mess / I can't get no rest / Oh man, so tired, so tired / But also totally wired, so wired*. I mean, that's all clichés, isn't it?"

"I spent hours on that!" said Ethan.

"What do *you* think?" said the singer, suddenly looking at me.

"Um . . . I think . . ." (Honest opinion: I thought that apart from the singer's voice, everything about the band, including the lyrics, was awful, all of it depressing, tuneless, and grating, but I knew that if I said anything negative about my brother's work I'd never be allowed in his bedroom again.) "... um ... it's edgy. In a good way. Like the music. You know. Very now."

A grunt of disagreement (or possibly agreement) (or gastric wind) emerged from behind the drum kit, but nobody paid it any attention.

"You know what?" said the singer, waving Freya's notebook through the air in front of her. "This right here is genius! Your little sister's a genius! Go again from the top. I want to try something."

"What are you talking about?" said Ethan.

"Just take it from the top."

"One ... two ... uh ... uh ..." yelled the drummer, and the song kicked off again. This time, instead of singing about misery, depression, and loneliness, the girl sang in a high, mournful soprano about a unicorn who loses his friends and climbs a rainbow to the moon, where he finds a palace made of marshmallows, to which all the lost animals of the world come. The unicorn serves every lost animal a drink from a fountain of magic raspberry juice, then sends them back down the rainbow, at the bottom of which every creature finds its missing loved one, and thus peace and tranquility are restored to the world.

The song came to an end.

"Woooooo hooooooooooooo!" yelled Freya. "That's just the best thing ever! You made my story into a song! It's awesome!"

"I love it!" said the singer, high-fiving Freya.

"That is pretty cool, actually," said Darius. "It's got something. I mean we're actually tapping into the psychedelia thing here, which is what we need for a USP."

"Mmm," said Ethan, though I could see he didn't know what a USP was, and was massively annoyed to find his seven-year-old sister's lyrics preferred to his own. "I dunno."

"What do you think?" Darius asked the drummer.

"S'okay," she said.

"What about you?" said the singer, looking at me. "It's cool the way the words work against the music, no?"

I find it hard to disagree with females who are mind-blowingly attractive, but, on the other hand, I couldn't bring myself to contribute to the ever more dominant idea that everyone in my family except me was some kind of genius. I wanted to point out that Freya was only seven and was clearly not a skilled lyricist, and that if anyone had asked me to write some certifiably bonkers story about unicorns and magic juice fountains and marshmallow palaces I could have done something lots better, but I knew there was no way of saying this that wouldn't make me sound like an ass. Nor did it seem wise to take the band's side against Ethan.

"Umm . . . I like both versions," I said.

The whole band rolled their eyes and turned away, as if I had somehow managed to find the only answer that annoyed everyone, so I decided to retreat to my room.

For the next hour, my ceiling pulsed and vibrated to the sound of the ongoing rehearsal. The new chorus, which went on and on, seemed to be:

Marshmallow palace flying high
I don't know where, I don't know why
This is my place of perfect love
My raspberry fountain high above.

For some reason, my brother's band using my sister's lyrics filled me with a surge of outrage and irritation that tipped the scales of my drama dilemma. I didn't know what the connection was, or if I was now somehow competing with a seven-year-old, but by the time the band packed up and left, I knew that if I was offered a part in the play I would take it.

The phrase "I'll show them" seemed to be rattling around somewhere in my brain, though who *they* were, and what it was I'd be showing them, I had no idea.

Me versus drool boy

The next morning, during homeroom, something extraordinary happened. I walked in and Jennifer spoke to me.

That's it.

Okay, it doesn't sound like much, but as far as I'm concerned this was my personal moon landing, Olympic gold medal, and World Cup–winning penalty kick all rolled into one.

Amazingly, there's more. She'd didn't just say hi. She told me that a notice was up, and I had a callback.

"Wow!" I said, mirroring her smile despite having no idea what on earth she was talking about.

"I got one too," she added, clapping her hands together in that I'm-so-happy-I-have-to-applaud-myself way I've never really understood.

"Great!" I said, hoping my eyes weren't giving away my ongoing total incomprehension of what we were discussing. "That's excellent."

"It looks like I'm down to the last five for Miranda, and you're up against three or four others for Caliban."

"Awesome! And Miranda is . . . ?"

"The female lead. Opposite Ferdinand, which Felipe's up for, obviously. He'll definitely get it."

The play! She was talking about the play!

I concentrated hard on pulling a face that wouldn't give away that I'd only just understood the topic of our conversation.

"Caliban's like a monster-type thing?" she added. "But my mom says it's a really cool part. Go and look at the notice."

"Okay. Good idea. And I guess I'll see you at the recall."

"The callback."

"The callback. That's what I meant."

"It's in batches. For each part."

"Oh, batches. Yeah, of course. Yeah. I always forget the batches. Batches, eh."

Realizing I was seriously overplaying my familiarity with callback batches, I turned and hurried from the room, bumping into Just Call Me Tony in the doorway.

"Hey hey hey! Haste makes waste," said Just Call Me Tony. "Where are you going? It's homeroom."

"I need to see the drama bulletin board. Jennifer says I've got a callout."

"A callout?"

"A callback," said Jennifer.

"A callback! Wow!" said Just Call Me Tony, putting down the felting kit he was carrying and giving my shoulder a fatherly squeeze. "That's great. You must be feeling really proud right now."

"Well, I need to see the notice."

"Okay. Off you go. And it's great to see you beginning to find your wings. I think you're on the cusp of some interesting personal developments, Sam."

I darted out of the room, pausing to stick a middle finger up at Just Call Me Tony through the wall, out of sight of the teacher I was insulting, but not, unfortunately, of Mrs. Florizel, who was standing right behind me.

When I turned and we found ourselves face-to-face, she gave me a severe teachery stare, though a hint of a smirk seemed to be playing at the corners of her mouth. I'm pretty sure I could see in her eyes something along the lines of *I have to tell this kid off, but I also think Just Call Me Tony is a dick and I can't wait to tell everyone in the staff room what just happened.*

"I saw that," she said.

I looked at the ground, faking remorse.

"It's healthy to express hard-to-verbalize emotions through physical movement, but gestures can be just as hurtful as words," she said.

I nodded.

"I'll look forward to seeing you bring to life some of your internal conflicts in my next class," she added. "There is a respectful and appropriate way to physicalize even the darkest thoughts. Harnessing inner trauma is key to releasing your full potential."

"Thanks, miss. I'll try," I said, rushing off toward the drama bulletin board before she could issue any punishment.

There, sure enough, was my name. It was on a list with three others, above an instruction to present ourselves for a second audition in the drama room at the end of the day. There were eight separate lists, each with a different thirty-minute slot. Jennifer was there, just before me, in a group with several of the most beautiful girls in the school, and Felipe was in another slot with the handsome gang. I only recognized one other name on my list—a guy in the year above me with a chin bigger than his forehead, volcanic acne, cauliflower ears, and an unexplained problem with drool.

I arrived early to size up the other monster-wannabes. Drool Boy was by far the ugliest. The other two looked relatively normal, though they both had an unsettling look in their eyes, which I guessed was either competitiveness or psychopathy. Or both, which was an unnerving combination given that we were all vying for the same part.

As we were called in, Jennifer and a cloud of fragrant hair-tossing girls wafted out into the corridor.

"Good luck!" she said to me.

"Why are you being nice?" I almost said—it was a burning question—but I managed to stop myself. Instead, I opted for a more appropriate "How did yours go?"

"All right, I think. Fingers crossed!"

She crossed her fingers at me. I crossed mine back.

This was bizarre. Was she treating me like a human being just because I was up for the school play? Had my comedy routine in the audition changed her opinion of me? Was it too outlandish to consider the possibility that she might have decided she actually liked me?

The phrase "zero to hero" sprang to mind, though in my case it was more like zero to 0.1. But still, that was progress. And if I could land a part in the school play, with Jennifer also in the cast, then maybe anything was possible. On a social acceptance scale of zero to ten, a 0.2 or 0.3 was beginning to look achievable.

Mr. Duverne began the audition with a movement exercise that was supposed to awaken our "animal nature." We were each given a section of the room and told to vocally and physically mark out our territory without using any human language.

I was useless, awkwardly and self-consciously recycling my monkey noises from the first audition, but the others were no better. One boy chose to use mouth farts as his method of communication, which didn't seem to impress Mr. Duverne.

After that, he sat us on the floor in a circle and told us that we were the last four in the running for Caliban, who would play a key role in his postcolonial reimagining of the play. We had been chosen because he'd seen in each of us the potential to harness the "wildness and otherness" essential to this character, who is an outsider, seen as monstrous by the aristocrats in the play, but who the audience needs to recognize as a victim of unjust oppression.

He then handed out a photocopied sheet and said we had five minutes to prepare a reading. I scanned it hurriedly, then slowed down to try to figure out what it meant. As far as I could tell, it was about a guy who's had an island nicked from him and is massively pissed off about it.

This island's mine, by Sycorax my mother,
Which thou takest from me. When thou camest first,
Thou strokedst me and madest much of me, wouldst give me

Water with berries in't, and teach me how
To name the bigger light, and how the less,
That burn by day and night: and then I loved thee
And show'd thee all the qualities o' the isle,
The fresh springs, brine-pits, barren place and fertile:
Cursed be I that did so! All the charms
Of Sycorax, toads, beetles, bats, light on you!
For I am all the subjects that you have,
Which first was mine own king: and here you sty me
In this hard rock, whiles you do keep from me
The rest o' the island.

Fart Mouth Kid was sent up first. He started by announcing, "My mom said I should tell you that I have some challenges understanding social cues, but I'm very good at memorizing things and I have eighth grade French horn."

"Thank you. That's good to know," replied Mr. Duverne.

"And I can also do accents. Scottish, Irish, German, Indian—"

"Let's not worry about accents just yet. Why don't you get started and give me the reading in your own voice."

His performance style was unusual, with a long pause for breath at the end of every line, and such a droning, robotic voice that I almost expected him to end with "If you want to hear these options again, press zero." I could tell by the look of serene disinterest in Mr. Duverne's eyes that, on top of the flatulence misjudgment, the social challenges diagnosis, and the talent for racist accents, this more or less ruled him out.

Drool Boy was next. He did a decent job of resembling a human being—which was a step up—but every time he got the to the letter *f* a spray of spittle flew outward, leaving glistening droplets on his oversize chin. He also pronounced the letter *s* with the sound people make when they're trying to cough up phlegm. The overall effect was less than beautiful.

The third guy didn't seem to understand what punctuation meant, and phrased every sentence as if it was a question. "This island's mine, by Sycorax my mother? Which thou takest from me? When thou camest first thou strokedst me? And madest much of me? Wouldst give me water with berries, isn't it? Hang on, it says 'I-N apostrophe T.' Is that, like, 'isn't' or 'in it'? Or is it just 'int'?"

"Thank you. Very good. I think that's all I need for now," said Mr. Duverne.

Then it was my turn, and I knew this part was there for the taking.

My heart accelerated to a distracting, chest-rumbling thud as I took my place at the center of the room. When I looked down to begin my reading, the paper was trembling in my hands. I refolded it, bending the bottom double to make the page flap less in my shaky grip.

I cleared my throat.

You can do this, I told myself. *You can do it. This is within reach.*

I cleared my throat again and began to read. I stopped at the periods. I paused at the commas. I attempted to sound as if I understood what I was saying. At the "in't" conundrum, I opted for "int."

When I looked up at the end, I saw what seemed very much like relief on the face of Mr. Duverne.

"Thank you," he said. "Excellent."

That was what he said after anyone performed anything, but this time it sounded like he actually meant it.

No such thing as a Goody One-shoe

"So how was everyone's day?" asked Mom.

The inevitable silence that followed this question never dented her enthusiasm for asking it every single time we sat down to dinner, like some kind of maternal version of a cuckoo clock.

Mom never gave up though.

"Freya? How was your day?"

"Okay."

"Did anything happen?"

"No."

"Nothing at all?"

"No."

"Tell me something. One thing that happened at school."

Freya looked at the ceiling for a few seconds, chewing ruminatively, then said, "There was a thing at playtime when Lucy called Jasper retarded and he got a stick and poked her and she screamed as if she'd basically been shot and told a teacher so Jasper went to the office and he was in huge trouble but when he said that she'd said he was retarded she was called in because you're not supposed to use that word especially not about Jasper because he actually is special needs or something anyway nobody knows what it is but he has extra classes with a tall woman who comes in on Tuesdays so then Lucy was in trouble and he wasn't in trouble but then she showed the bruise which meant they were both in trouble even though Lucy's a real Goody Two-shoes and never gets in trouble even though she actually should because when the teachers aren't looking she says really mean things to people then acts all upset if they say it back. I think there's something wrong with her not actually special needs but just kind of evil or something not because of what she says but because of the way she pretends to the teachers that she's the opposite of what she really is as in *mean*. And why is a Goody Two-shoes called a Goody Two-shoes, anyway? I mean who wears one shoe? Nobody."

"Wow!" said Mom. "That's quite a story."

"Long John Silver," said Ethan.

"What?" said Mom.

"One shoe," said Ethan.

"But he's a bad guy," said Freya. "He'd be a Baddy One-shoe."

"What about you, Ethan?" said Mom, cutting off the conversation about amputees (so to speak). "How was your day?"

"Okay."

"Oh, not you as well! Tell me something! I'm not just here to cook and clean up after you."

"You don't clean up after me. We have a cleaner."

"Don't be facetious," said Mom.

"You're old enough to clean up after yourself, Ethan," said Dad, who liked to occasionally register his presence by saying boring and/or annoying things.

"Just tell us about your day," said Mom.

"Well, there's a thing with Darius. His dad's in the music business. He's a . . . I don't know what he is . . . a producer or something . . . anyway, Darius knows everyone, and the band's getting better, so he says he's going to set up a showcase. Which is like a gig, but with music business people invited. And if they like you, they sign you."

"Coooool!" said Mom. "That's amazing! Awesome!"

"Is that after your midterms?" said Dad.

"Can't you think of something positive to say first?" said Mom.

"I'm pleased. It's good. But is it after your midterms?"

"God, Dad. You're such a downer!"

"That's really exciting, Ethan. I'm so proud," said Mom.

"I wrote one of the songs," said Freya.

"Of course you did," said Mom, clearly not believing her.

"It's true," said Ethan. "We're using one of her stories as lyrics. They're kind of trippy."

"Really?"

"Yeah. It wasn't my idea. It was Cass."

"A family collaboration! How lovely!" said Mom.

"Is Cass a person?" said Dad, who often lagged so far behind in family conversations it was like the rest of us had lapped him.

"No, she's a brand of detergent," said Ethan, employing the kind of sarcasm even a sledgehammer would find unsubtle.

"What?" said Dad.

"She's the singer," said Mom.

"The beautiful one?" asked Dad.

"Yeah. I suppose so. If you're into that kind of thing," said Ethan.

"If you're into that kind of thing?" said Dad. "She's a knockout! You can't say you haven't noticed! I mean . . . not that *I've* particularly noticed, but . . . I'm just surprised you haven't . . . but . . . I mean, obviously, if you're heterosexual, which you're not . . . which is fine . . . not a problem at all . . . anyway, I just mean, men who happen not to be in the LGBT community . . . for most of us it's hard not to notice when a woman is . . . um . . . just in aesthetic terms . . . striking. Good bone structure. That's all I'm saying. Anyway, who wants more pasta?"

Mom stared at him, unimpressed. Dad looked down and began to concentrate intently on his next mouthful of food.

"Have you taught *Dad* the secret code!?" said Freya, her little face suddenly all crumpled and wounded.

"No. I really haven't," said Ethan.

"What about you, Sam? What's your news?" asked Mom.

For once, I actually had an answer. "I think I might have gotten into the school play," I said.

"You?" said Dad. "I mean—you! Great! Excellent!"

"I thought you hate all that," said Ethan.

"I decided to give it a try," I said.

"Did you practice for the audition with Jennifer?" asked Mom.

"No. Turned out to be not that kind of audition."

"Ah, Jennifer!" said Ethan. "That explains it."

"Who's Jennifer?" asked Dad.

"You'd like her," said Ethan. "Good bone structure."

"What's a bone structure?" asked Freya.

"The point is, I did the audition and I got through to the second round, which was today, and I think I did okay."

"Do I have one?" asked Freya.

"That is sooooooo good," said Mom. "Awesome! But you shouldn't be too disappointed if you don't get it."

"You're assuming someone else will be better than me?"

"NO!" said Mom. "That's the last thing I meant!"

"Can't you think of something positive to say?" said Dad, to Mom.

"What's that supposed to mean?" she snapped back.

"I think you'll get it, Sam," said Dad, giving me a wink. "I'm right behind you."

"Why are you winking?" said Mom. "What does that mean?"

"I can't do anything right, can I?!" barked Dad, slamming his cutlery down.

A tense silence descended.

"I can wink!" said Freya, bravely attempting to lighten the atmosphere with an on-the-spot demonstration.

It turned out she couldn't wink, after all.

"Has it crossed anyone's mind to maybe ask about *my* day?" said Mom.

We all looked at her, but for some reason it still didn't occur to any of us to actually ask about her day.

She pressed on though, as if we had. "I've decided

pottery isn't the outlet I've been looking for. I'm selling the kiln and installing traditional woodworking equipment. I'm going to make Japanese stools!"

She made the stools announcement as if this was big news.

Our response was underwhelming. In fact, there wasn't one.

"I've fallen in love with a particular Kyoto butterfly design. I've learned a lot from clay, but I think wood might be my soul element."

"That's great. Stools! Wow! Excellent idea," said Dad, but I could see him mentally ticking the "say something positive" box.

A feeling continued to hang over the table that there was something else we were supposed to be saying, but nobody had any idea what it was.

"Is wood an element?" I said eventually.

"I might look up the periodic table and see if I can find wood on it," said Ethan, pulling his phone from his pocket.

"Japanese stools!" said Dad. "What a lovely idea."

"So have you ordered a stool sample from Japan to copy?" asked Ethan.

For some reason this made Dad laugh and Mom walk out of the room.

"I think you should go and apologize," said Dad, after forcing himself to stop laughing.

"*You* apologize! You're the one that cracked up," said Ethan.

In the end, neither of them apologized. They finished eating instead.

Mom spent the rest of the evening shut away in her office/studio/den, tapping furiously into her laptop. At bedtime I took a sneaky look at her blog, which now had a long rant about the male urge to quash female creativity, including an epic moan about how hard it was to produce the unceasing flow of love, nurture, and encouragement that is expected of a mother, when all your teenage sons return is mockery, ingratitude, and cynicism.

I was used to feeling annoyed and slandered by Mom's blog posts, but this time I felt something different. It started as a heavy sensation in my chest, a dull ache I couldn't identify, then it spread and intensified. After a few minutes I realized this is what it felt like to have a pang of conscience.

If you've never had one, it's kind of hard to describe. The feeling is a little bit like the one you get just after you've eaten past-their-sell-by-date shrimp: a clenching of the stomach, mingled with waves of foreboding and regret.

I reread the blog, and the feeling got worse. Even though it had only just been posted, there were already a few short comments underneath, saying things like, "Too true!" and "Stay strong! xx."

I tapped my finger in the box for sending a response and watched the cursor flash there for a while. A long while.

Eventually, I wrote, "I'm sorry we were rude about your carpentry. I'm looking forward to seeing what you make. S xx."

Then I deleted it.

Then I wrote it again.

Then I deleted it, wrote it once more, and hit Send.

Felipe's little black book in his head

Only twenty-four hours after being pleasantly surprised that Jennifer had even greeted me, I walked into my homeroom and she let out a friend-scream (the scream girls give to celebrate the arrival of a BFF, not the a-serial-killer-has-jumped-out-of-my-cupboard scream you see in horror movies). As I was turning my head to see who was behind me in the doorway, she launched herself at me and without any warning administered what can only be described as a hug. Luckily, this was so unexpected and disorienting that I didn't have time to get an erection.

"WE'RE IN!" she said, stepping back and beaming at me. "BOTH OF US! I'm Miranda and you're Caliban!"

"Wow! That's great!" I said, spreading my arms in the hope this might instigate another embrace, now that my brain had sufficiently caught up with events for me to be capable of enjoying it.

"All three of us!"

"Three?"

"Yeah! Felipe's going to be Ferdinand. The romantic lead. Isn't that great?"

"Uh . . . yeah."

Marina, wearing what for her counted as a relatively staid outfit (an army jacket, a tutu, stripy tights, and yellow Doc Martens), must have been listening in on our conversation, because she appeared between us, smiling proudly, and said, "I'm doing the costumes."

"*You?*" said Jennifer.

"Yeah."

"For the play?"

"Yeah. Designing them and everything."

"You?"

"Yes."

Jennifer eyed her up and down skeptically.

"So what am I going to be wearing?" she asked.

"I haven't started yet."

"Is it up to you?"

"And Mr. Duverne. We're going to work it out together."

"It's not going to be something weird, is it?"

"I don't know."

"'Cause Miranda's the love interest, so it's important that everyone thinks she's cute. She has to look innocent, but also really hot, but not in a slutty way. Kind of sexy but virginal."

"Like a ripe cherry?" said Marina.

"Exactly!" said Jennifer.

"You want to look like a sexy, virginal cherry?"

"Not literally! Apparently I'm a symbol. For the West."

"The West? All of it?"

"I think so. It's about postcolonialism. I'm the White Man's Burden."

"What's that?"

"I don't know."

At this point, Felipe walked in. Jennifer turned away from Marina and me, screamed, and threw herself at him. Holding her close, he said, "I'm really looking forward to playing opposite you. It's going to be really intense."

"Yeah," she said.

Still holding her around the waist, he said, "We're going to have to fall in love onstage. We mustn't let that affect our friendship."

"Of course."

"We've been friends a long time. And I know we dated ages ago, when we were ten . . ."

"And twelve."

"Yeah, and again when we were twelve. But we're going

to have to be really professional and find a way to get into these roles without feeling self-conscious. You know?"

"Yeah. Of course," she said, for some reason doing an awful lot of blinking.

"Cool. I'm going to have to phone my agent."

"Sam's in too," said Jennifer. "He's Caliban."

Felipe let go of Jennifer and turned toward me. "The monster?" he said.

"Mr. Duverne says Caliban's going to be the moral center of a postcolonial reinterpretation," I replied.

Felipe stepped closer, putting me within his pungent personal cloud of aftershave and styling mousse. "You screwed me in that audition, shitbag," he said. "So you'd better watch out. Felipe has a little black book in his head, and he never forgets."

What God had given Felipe by way of looks, he'd held back in the intelligence department.

"You have a book inside your head?" I replied. "Is that really the best place to keep it?"

"You screw me, I screw you. That's how it works," said Felipe, tapping his temple.

"You're a fast mover," I said. "We haven't even been on a date yet."

For a delicious second, Jennifer and Marina laughed, but both girls were swiftly silenced by an angry stare from Felipe.

"I've got my eye on you," he said, turning back to face me, pouting vigorously. "If you push me too far, you'll regret it."

Turning his body, then his head, he spun away from me and strutted to his desk, with Jennifer close behind.

Marina shot me an I-can't-believe-that-just-happened frown followed by a Felipe-is-an-epic-tool shake of the head.

I shrugged in agreement.

"Yo, people!" said Just Call Me Tony, entering the room carrying a harp. "Attendance! Who's not here? Anyone? Okay, cool—now—forgiveness! Compassion! Loving-kindness! Pretty sappy words, huh? But what if we direct them inward? I'm spitballing here, but let's throw some ideas in the ring and see what happens if we work toward writing a letter of forgiveness to *ourselves*. Mmkay? Let's think about that. Mmkay?"

First rehearsal was immediately after school the next day. Mr. Duverne had set up a long table in the middle of the drama room, marked out with name tags for each character. He gave us each a copy of the play and told us to find our seats. Main characters were at the center, bit parts at either end. I was roughly halfway down.

Mr. Duverne started with a long speech about how we had all been carefully chosen after exhaustive thought, and how being in the play was a huge privilege; then we began a read-through of the play.

It was very long. It didn't make a huge amount of sense. There were lots of drippy and tedious scenes between Jennifer and Felipe. Half my scenes were (I think) supposed to be comedy, but I couldn't tell if my character was intended as hideous or ridiculous or funny or pitiful or all four. My story line was about me being the revolting, deformed son of a hideous witch, working as a slave on a desert island until I meet someone who seems to offer me a better life, but this turns out to be a joke, and at the end I have to accept that I was an idiot for thinking I could ever be anything other than a scumbag.

Jennifer didn't have to do much more than waft around the stage being in love, while Felipe's job was to be a douchey dreamboat and suck up to Jennifer's dad in the hope that he'd allow him to get it on with his foxy daughter.

Jennifer's dad—Prospero—is a Dumbledore-type old wizard guy who controls everything. He was played by a senior guy called Ulf, whose grandfather was reputed to have invented Pilates, and whose mom supposedly competed in the Olympic high jump for Norway before becoming a model and then a conceptual artist. Ulf was such a good actor he could even make Shakespeare sound like it made sense.

At the end of the read-through we all gave ourselves a round of applause, Mr. Duverne made a long speech about the journey we were embarking on, then we filed out, everyone chatting excitedly.

Just outside the school gates, Francine was waiting for Jennifer in a vast car that looked like a cross between a VIP lounge and an armored personnel carrier. She waved down at me from her high-altitude driver's seat, lowered her window, congratulated me on getting into the play, and offered me a lift.

"Okay. Thanks," I said, climbing in. Literally climbing.

After a protracted farewell hug with Felipe, Jennifer got in behind me and the door *thunk*ed shut, enclosing us in a pristine leather-scented cocoon.

"So! Caliban!" said Francine, pulling out into traffic without using her turn signal, or even waiting for a gap. Oblivious to the sound of screeching tires and a blaring horn, she began to enthuse about my part in the play. "Magnificent role! Poor Jennifer will just have to stand around looking pretty, but you've really got something to sink your teeth into. I'll make sure I bring my agent to the opening night. This really is a wonderful opportunity for you. It's such a thrill as an actor to channel something monstrous. To really dig deep! Mr. Duverne must be hugely impressed with you. For a young actor this is a glorious springboard."

Jennifer, sensing that nobody other than Francine would be required to speak for the duration of the journey, spent the drive looking at her phone, while I periodically opened my mouth to answer the questions Francine threw at me, only for Francine to answer them herself, or move on to yet more questions. It was like trying to make conversation with a hand dryer.

"Hugs to your mom!" she said as we pulled up outside my house.

I jumped swiftly down from the car, taking stock of a lesson learned: even though a lift from Francine offered precious proximity to Jennifer, it was better to walk.

The ... thing

Mom never mentioned the comment I left on her blog, but I know she saw it, because for a few days it felt like there was a thaw between us. I'd never doubted that she loved me, but it now seemed as if she actually liked me too. Which made me wonder if maybe I also liked her. Occasionally I found myself just hanging out with her in the kitchen, chatting. It was all rather bizarre.

Then she began to get sucked into her Japanese stool project, and the whole atmosphere of the house changed. For a week she barely emerged from her studio, which was now renamed as a "workshop." From early morning till late at night the garden was filled with the traditional Japanese sounds of nailing, sawing, sandpapering, and swearing. On the rare occasions when Mom was spotted in the house, each time she seemed to be wearing a new bandage on a different finger. Her face took on the hangdog pallor of a recently bereaved orphan. The fridge was bare. Meals were self-service.

Then, one evening, just as we were sitting down to our third takeout dinner of the week, Mom appeared in the kitchen, her cheeks aglow with pride, carrying a . . . thing.

She placed it proudly and reverentially in the center of the room.

I didn't want to be the first one to ask if it was a stool.

Nor, it appeared, did anyone else.

There was a long silence.

"So that's the stool!" said Freya, with an intonation that was roughly three-quarters exclamation mark and only one-quarter question mark.

"Yes!" said Mom, all exclamation mark.

There was another long silence.

"Have you tried it yet?" asked Freya.

"No," said Mom. "Would you like to be the first?"

Freya's face froze in the expression you get when you've just mistaken salt for sugar. Clearly, she did not want to be the first. The . . . thing . . . was so uneven, so spiky and rickety-looking, and so hideously ugly that it wasn't even obvious which part of it you were supposed to sit on. How this could call itself a butterfly stool when it bore no resemblance to a butterfly, and equally little resemblance to a stool, was a mystery. The chances of it holding together under the weight of a seven-year-old child looked slim.

"Go on, then," said Mom, who appeared to have mistaken Freya's obvious reluctance for a "yes, please."

"You made it," said Freya. "Maybe you should take the first turn."

"No, no. I want to see how it looks. I'd love you to have the honor."

This was a very strange use of the word "honor."

Freya warily began to reverse herself toward the . . . thing. With tense thighs, she lowered herself onto it, bracing herself for a collapse. There was a creaking noise and a curious *squeak*, but no catastrophic implosion.

"Relax," said Mom. "Enjoy it!"

Freya released some of the tension from her legs, putting a shade more weight on to the stool. "Mmm," she said. "Comfy!" Then she swiftly bounced up and gave Mom the kind of hug that allows you to congratulate someone while concealing your facial expression. "It's so perfect I don't think you ever need to make another one," she added, which perhaps wasn't quite as subtle as she thought it was.

"Who's next?" said Mom.

Dad, Ethan, and me all became suddenly engrossed in our pizzas.

"Sam?" said Mom.

"Um . . . I've just gotten into the school play so I can't . . ." I was about to say that I couldn't risk a major spinal injury but realized this might sound tactless, so I cunningly changed course. "I mean . . . just, all the rehearsals have made me really hungry. So I'm . . . you know . . . still eating."

"Ethan?"

"Starving! Absolutely famished!" he said, reaching out and taking the last slice.

"So it's you, then," said Mom, smiling tensely at Dad. She had clearly begun to notice the general aura of skepticism toward her woodworking competence.

"Me?" said Dad.

"Yes. Go on."

"But . . . I'm the heaviest."

"It's fine. It can take up to three hundred pounds," said Mom.

"Really?"

"That's what the instructions say."

"Ah," said Dad. "Right." The question of whether this . . . thing . . . looked anything like the stool in the instructions was not one that could be asked. The stakes were too high.

"Go on, then," said Mom.

Dad planted his hands on his thighs, raised himself from his solid, factory-made dining chair, and took three heavy, reluctant steps toward Mom's . . . thing.

He hovered over it.

"Three hundred pounds, you say?" he asked.

"Yup."

"It's so beautiful," he said. "Could we just hang it on the wall as a work of art? I mean, it seems a shame to use it."

"I know exactly what you mean," said Mom, "but I've been reading a lot about beauty and functionality, and that's what drew me toward Japanese design in the first place."

"What does that mean?" asked Dad.

"It means you have to sit on it," said Ethan.

"Okay," said Dad. "Great. Now?"

"Yes," said Mom. "Now."

Dad bent his knees. He lowered his backside. It touched the wood. He squatted tensely, bum-to-stool, like someone miming sitting down on a nonexistent chair. "Lovely!" he said. "Really comfortable. Great design!"

I could see his leg muscles trembling under the strain.

"Relax into it," said Mom. "Let yourself go."

Dad eased more weight onto the . . . thing. It began to creak, more loudly than under Freya's weight. Unlike with Freya, the creaking didn't stop once he was settled. Instead it grew into an ominous cracking, splitting sound. Then the cracking, splitting sound grew into a sudden noisy *snap* as the . . . thing . . . shattered into several pieces, sending Dad sprawling onto the kitchen floor.

After a brief volley of swearing, silence descended on the room. Nobody moved or spoke. We all looked at Mom, who was gazing at the site of her woodworking disaster with the stare of someone who simply cannot believe what they have just seen.

"Don't mind me!" said Dad eventually, scrambling to his feet. "I'm fine! No major fractures."

"How much is it you weigh?" asked Mom.

"Less than three hundred pounds! It almost broke when Freya sat on it!"

"I'm going upstairs to do some breathing," said Mom, walking slowly but purposefully out of the room. "I don't want to be disturbed."

Ethan was the first to laugh: silently, with a fist in his mouth, his whole body shaking uncontrollably. I lost it next, then Freya, then Dad. None of us dared make a sound, but Freya ended up rolling on the floor, and Dad was literally weeping. So there was an upside, after all, to the Japanese woodwork debacle.

It's a bonding and uplifting experience for a whole family to laugh together over a shared joke. This wasn't actually the whole family, and the fact that we were all laughing at Mom was maybe a notch or two down from true domestic harmony, but you can't have everything.

* * *

Meanwhile, my rehearsals for the play were going about as well as Mom's carpentry. Mr. Duverne called me in on my own at first, for a session to help me "inhabit the part of Caliban." I tried my best, but I felt self-conscious and could tell I was disappointing him.

He kept on asking me to "channel the energy you found in the first audition," but that performance had been fueled by the feeling of getting an audience on my side and making them laugh at a guy I hated, combined with a strange nothing-to-lose freedom that came from temporarily not caring how I looked or whether I was getting things wrong. On my own, in a quiet room with a starey drama teacher, rehearsing a part I would have to perform in front of hundreds of people, that fearlessness vanished. All my inhibitions returned. I felt embarrassed by the uselessness of my own acting, which made me even worse and more embarrassed. I simply couldn't do it.

My first rehearsal with other actors was with Ulf and Jennifer, for a scene at the start of the play in which I crawl out of a rock, they tell me I'm disgusting, I shout lots of curses at them, then they both tell me what an asshole I am because they tried to be nice to me until I "didst seek to violate the honor" of Miranda, after which—fair play if you ask me—they chucked me out of the house and sent me to live in a cave. So it's safe to say I wasn't the romantic lead.

Ulf and Jennifer, without any apparent effort, seemed to know how to perform their lines. I didn't have a clue. I didn't know where to stand, how to speak, how to walk, or where to look. I didn't know anything.

Arms were a particular issue. Normally they just hang there from my shoulders, pick things up for me, then disappear from my awareness when they're not needed, but the minute you start acting, something weird happens to arms. Suddenly they're huge, and they flap around next to you, getting in the way and feeling like they're always in the wrong place, sending constant messages to your brain, screaming, "WHERE DO YOU WANT TO PUT ME NOW? HERE? HERE? LIKE THIS? DO YOU WANT ME TO GESTICULATE? OR JUST DANGLE? THIS DOESN'T FEEL RIGHT! NOR DOES THAT! NO, THIS IS WRONG TOO. PUT ME SOMEWHERE! TELL ME WHERE TO GO! WHERE DO YOU WANT ME TO GO!?"

This was kind of distracting.

My limbs were only a small problem, however, compared to the other big difficulty: talking. Remembering words and getting them out of my mouth in the right order. In a voice that gave the impression I understood what I was saying. That, I realized, was the major challenge in the acting field, and I didn't have any idea how to do it.

Two weeks into rehearsals, Mr. Duverne took me aside and told me he was "feeling a lot of resistance." When I asked him what this meant, he said, "I need to know if you really want to be in this play. Because if you don't, I'll find someone else."

The audition had been a fluke. Acting was clearly not my area. A moment of random overexcitement had deluded me into succumbing to some kind of crazy, egotistical ambition to prove myself in a field where—as I had always known in my heart of hearts—I had no talent, and no gift. Unless I reconnected to the personality-transforming spell that had been cast over me in the audition, my performance would be a disaster.

"You think I'm going to be garbage, don't you?" I said.

"I think if you're not ready to make a sincere effort, you don't belong in this cast," he replied.

Was that the problem? Was I just not trying hard enough?

I couldn't tell. Did I actually *want* to act? Did I like the idea of being up onstage with people looking at me, listening to me, and judging me? Or should I have known all along that I was someone whose place was in the back-ground, out of the limelight, watching others strut and perform?

Perhaps all those voices telling me to make an effort to fit in had in fact been leading me away from my true self, toward a dangerous lie, toward a fake version of myself who would be horribly exposed to the whole school the moment I took the stage.

"Well?" said Mr. Duverne.

"I don't know," I replied.

"'I don't know' isn't good enough. Sleep on it. Give me a proper answer tomorrow."

Ethan's next big confession

At home, that evening, something amazing happened. I was sitting in my room doing my homework, when Ethan walked in and flopped down on my bed.

If you don't know how bizarre that is, you've never had an older brother. The normal pattern of events was the other way around, with me going into his room, where I'd be greeted with either immediate dismissal, brief indulgence followed by dismissal, or affection expressed through the medium of physical violence followed by forcible ejection.

For him to enter my room for any reason other than to pass on a parental message was unprecedented.

"Are you okay?" I asked.

"NO!" he replied.

I put down my pen. Things were getting stranger. I was beginning to suspect that he wanted . . . a conversation.

"What's wrong?" I said.

"Everything."

"Everything?"

"Everything! Maybe I should just kill myself!"

He did not say this like someone with even the remotest intention of killing himself. His tone was unmistakably that of a teenage boy wallowing in melodramatic misery and slightly enjoying it. I know. I've been there.

"Why? What happened?" I asked.

"I can't eat. I can't sleep."

"You ate quite a lot at dinner. You had three helpings."

"I didn't enjoy it! Every mouthful tasted like dust. I can't play guitar anymore. Even music gives me no pleasure. I've died inside."

"What's happened?"

"I'm lovesick."

"Lovesick? Is that a real thing?"

"Yes! It's torture!"

"How did you catch it? I mean, who's the other person?"

"You can't tell anyone. It's a total secret. Nobody."

"Is it Cass?"

"How did you know?"

"Because it's obvious."

"Is it?"

"Totally."

"It can't be!"

"Why not?"

"Because I'm supposed to be gay! Everyone still thinks I'm gay. That's why I'm talking to you. You're the only one who knows I'm straight."

"What about Cass? Does she know?"

"I'm not sure. I think she thinks I'm bi. Because we had a thing."

"A thing?"

"I sort of . . . we were alone together and something just took me over and I put my arms around her and then we stared at each other for ages, and next thing I knew we were kissing. Then Veronika walked in and went ballistic."

"Veronika?"

"The drummer."

"Why did she go ballistic?"

"Because Cass is her girlfriend. She said we'd both betrayed her, then she started throwing her drums around and telling us she was quitting the band. Thing is, she's an amazing drummer, but I reckon what makes her so good is basically rage, probably against her parents, who are massively uptight and repressed and in denial about the fact that their only child so obviously has not one single heterosexual bone in her body. And usually she takes all this out on her drum kit. Which is great. But it's not a good idea to get on the wrong side of her. Or drummers in general—it's best not to get into arguments with them—and it's never a good idea to get caught making out with their girlfriends. Anyway, the point is, if Veronika leaves the band the whole thing's over, because all the equipment is hers. The amps, the speakers, the mikes, everything. Her dad's a hedge fund something-or-other. He basically farts money. Constantly. Without Veronika we'd have to go acoustic, and acoustic alt-metal psychedelia just doesn't work."

"So the band's finished?"

"No, Cass told her the kiss was an accident and didn't mean anything, even though if you ask me it meant *everything*. It meant more than any other thing I have ever done in my entire life. So the practice was canceled and Veronika stormed off, and she's been sulking all week, but Cass has told me that she thinks she's talked her around and the band is back together."

"Then why are you so depressed?"

"Because Cass says nothing can ever happen between us again or Veronika will blow the whole thing up."

"So is Cass gay?"

"She says she's questing."

"Questing?"

"She thinks gender is an artificial construct."

"I . . . um . . ."

"She doesn't want to be defined."

"What does that even mean?"

"I DON'T KNOW! I DON'T KNOW! I DON'T KNOW! It's all such a mess! Now I have to rehearse with her, knowing there's something between us, but not really knowing how much she's feeling, and looking for signs all the time that she does at least feel something, which is torture because neither of us can let anything show. Everything has to be completely suppressed and hidden away, except for just the tiniest secret glances. Which maybe I'm imagining! It's like being stuck in some awful uptight costume drama."

"Is it? Which one?"

"Not one in particular. I just mean all the repression. I've got the love that dare not speak its name!"

"What, liking a bisexual gender-questing singer in a rock band while pretending unconvincingly to be gay?"

"What do you mean, 'unconvincingly'?"

"Well, it's pretty unconvincing if you're going around making out with girls."

"Nobody knows about that. And it's only one girl."

"I'm just saying I don't find it very convincing."

"Well, you're the only one! Maybe when the band breaks up I'll come out as straight. I don't think I can do it much longer."

"Mom will be heartbroken."

"That's not my problem. I feel like I'm going crazy."

"You sound like you've already gone crazy."

"I'm completely trapped. Veronika watches me like a hawk! She doesn't trust me."

"I wonder why."

"What am I going to do? I feel like I'm constantly about to explode."

"That's normal, isn't it? Have you tried . . . ?"

"Don't be disgusting. Anyway, that doesn't help."

"Well, just don't kill yourself. Maybe go downstairs and have some cookies instead."

"I might do that."

"Or since they'll only taste of dust, maybe you could save some money and snack on the vacuum bag instead."

"Funny. You're a funny guy."

"Bring me some!" I yelled, as he left the room.

"Get them yourself," he replied, which I chose to take as his thank-you for our fraternal heart-to-heart.

The next day a van arrived and took away all Mom's woodworking equipment. She announced over dinner that her shed, previously a studio, was no longer to be referred to as a workshop. It was now a meditation space and multifunctional creative hub.

The day after that another van pulled up, with the words "Luigi's Ethnic Rhythm Emporium: Beats Working for a Living" written on the side. A man with a wiry gray ponytail, dressed in what can only be described as a vertical carpet, emerged and deposited an array of global percussion instruments in Mom's multifunctional creative hub: bongos, Indian drums, African drums, tambourines, a couple of xylophones, maracas, gongs, cymbals, bells, rain sticks, drumsticks, and things that looked like just stick sticks. On and on the delivery went, many of the objects utterly unidentifiable.

This was ominous, to say the least. I looked at her blog for an explanation of what was going on, but she didn't appear to have updated it since the Japanese-stool-implosion rant.

Over dinner, after a not very successful demonstration of how to play a Zambian thumb piano, she told us some friends would be visiting on Sunday for a workshop, and they shouldn't be disturbed.

"I'm confused," said Ethan. "You said we weren't supposed to call it a workshop any more."

"You're not."

"But you just said it was."

"I didn't. I said we're *having* a workshop."

"But not in a workshop?"

"Are you being facetious?"

"No. I'm just asking," he said, pulling his innocent face.

Mom looked skeptical.

"What's 'having a workshop'?" asked Freya.

"It's . . . well . . . a workshop can be a place where you work, or it can also mean something else, which is what's happening on Sunday, when you invite your friends over and you find a private space, and you talk about your feelings, and maybe play the drums a bit, or do some trust exercises, and just spend time being open and connecting with people who are important to you."

"Like a playdate?"

Mom's face stiffened, but she managed a tight smile. "A bit like that, yes."

"Are you going to have a workshop with your friends, Daddy?"

Ethan spluttered out a badly suppressed snigger. Dad pinched his lips together, took a deep breath through his nose, then said, "I don't have one on the calendar at the moment, but it does sound like a lot of fun."

He didn't look at Mom, even though she was staring at him extremely hard.

My high-risk Siberia dodge

The next morning I went to see Mr. Duverne in his office and promised him I would try harder. He seemed pleased, but then he was an actor, so it's just as possible that he was in fact crushingly disappointed not to get rid of me.

Did I have any idea how I would set about trying harder? Did I have any renewed confidence in my acting abilities, or a surge of desire to conquer my role and step out in front of an admiring audience? No, but I sensed that being cast in the play had given me the beginnings of an escape route from my nonperson status. Even Jennifer had, at long last, noticed my existence. Sometimes she was actually nice to me. You could almost say we'd become friends.

Walking out of the play would be a one-way ticket back to social Siberia. Giving up on this would be giving up on everything. It would be like crawling into a hole and letting life become something that happened to other people. Even if I was a terrible actor, even if I found the whole thing excruciating and embarrassing, I had to fight on.

At first, rehearsals were in small groups, scene by scene. Only when work started on the finale, which featured the entire cast, did we all get together again. And when we did, the inevitable happened. Or, rather, the inevitable had already happened, but this was when I noticed.

It's important for the leading actors in a love story to have what is known as "sexual chemistry." The romantic leads in our play were Jennifer and Felipe, and the minute I saw them onstage together, doing one of their sappy scenes, it was apparent that they'd gone way beyond chemistry, and into biology. They couldn't keep their hands off each other.

Offstage, they spent their time enacting even more sickly love scenes of their own devising, consisting of hand-holding, whispering, stroking, giggling, and a significant amount of frankly quite inappropriate groping. This was even more depressing to watch than the subtitled movies that Ethan pretended to like.

Life can be so cruel. But not to people like Felipe.

One of the strangest things about the human mind is that the more you don't want to see something, the more your brain makes you look at it. After a couple of awkward eye-contact incidents, I realized that I had to force myself to look anywhere other than where I kept finding myself staring, which was at the hideous, galling, nauseating sight of Jennifer and Felipe canoodling. I still found myself sneaking occasional peeks though, and when I accidentally caught Felipe's eye a third time in one rehearsal, I was horrified to see that he didn't just turn away, but began to walk toward me.

I peered meaningfully at the ceiling as he approached, trying to give the impression I was the kind of person who often found myself so deep in thought that I wasn't particularly aware of where my gaze happened to fall.

"Jealous?" said Felipe, which was not a greeting I'd ever received before.

I gave a small start of surprise, as if I hadn't noticed him approach, and countered with the wittiest riposte I could think of: "What?"

"You can't stop staring. I get that a lot, but you're making Jennifer feel awkward. If you don't want to freak her out, I think you need to quit."

"Staring?"

Felipe sat down next to me and placed a pseudo-affectionate hand on my shoulder. "Listen, pal," he said. "Losing hurts. I know that. Not from personal experience, obviously, but I've heard. Anyway, you were dreaming if you ever thought Jennifer might be interested in you. So just forget it, and try to remember who you are."

"Who I am?"

"I'm not calling you a loser. Nobody should be put in a box. Labels aren't for people. They're for ... um ... clothes. Yeah? I'm just saying you need to find your level. And listen, I know everyone who's got scenes with you has been saying how crap your acting is, and talking you down and stuff, but I want you to know that I'm behind you. I think you've got glimmers of potential and you're not going to be nearly as bad as everyone says. So I'm with you, man. And if you want any acting tips, don't be shy to ask."

"Is that what everyone's saying?"

"Hey, I'm not one to break confidences. That's not how I roll. But him and him and him and her and her and her over there were all talking about you earlier and it wasn't pretty. The important thing is, you can't let it affect your confidence. Confidence is half the battle. And I should probably tell you there's a guy from one of the top theater agencies who wants to represent me, and he's coming to see the show. So don't screw up any of my scenes on opening night. Okay? Or I'll kill you."

"Okay."

"And don't tell my agent."

"That you threatened to kill me?"

"No—that there's another agent coming. It's a secret. If she knows I'm window-shopping for better representation she'll flip."

"Um . . . okay."

"Listen—I know how you feel. I mean, I can guess what it probably feels like to be rejected by a girl. Jennifer's amazing, but you have to forget about her. Because the way you keep staring at us just makes you seem like a creeper. There'll be a girl that's right for you. Somewhere. One day. You don't have to be physically attractive to do well with girls if you have the right personality, so all you need to do is change your personality and you'll stand a chance. Not with Jennifer, obviously, but with someone. Hopefully. Anyway, it's been good to chat. I hope it's helped. See you around."

With that, he swiveled and walked—no, strutted—back to Jennifer, who was busily looking away as if unaware that Felipe had just crossed the room to crush my life under the heel of his cowboy boot.

How on earth could anyone want to be with someone like him?

How on earth could someone like Felipe get through life without getting beaten up every day?

Surely, at some point, Jennifer would notice that her boyfriend was a despicable human being lacking any shred of modesty, compassion, intelligence, or decency. Eventually, that had to count against you.

Moments after our friendly, confidence-boosting chat, I was called up onstage for a scene. This was the first time I'd had to perform in front of the whole cast.

I was awful. Worse than ever. An average floorboard would have been less wooden. Mr. Duverne watched me with the same look of revulsion and pity you might give a dog lapping up vomit. Nobody else quite matched Mr. Duverne's level of dismay, but I could sense that everyone had heard the gossip about my performance, and they were all now seeing firsthand that it was true. Only one person was smiling: Felipe.

Leather Speedos

With a week to go before the first full run-through, I was told to go for a "wardrobe meeting" with Marina. We met in a windowless room in a distant corner of the drama department that was crammed with racks of clothes and pungent with the scent of mothballs, dusty velvet, and stage makeup. When I walked in, Marina was sewing under an anglepoise lamp, wearing an asymmetrical jumpsuit plastered with alien encounter scenes cut out of old comics, looking as happy as I'd ever seen her.

Because of her taste in clothes I'd initially thought Marina was one of the most pretentious, attention-seeking people in my class (and there was stiff competition), but as the year progressed, and I saw how she made zero effort to suck up to the people who thought they were cool, I realized I'd been wrong about her. She wasn't, in fact, wearing look-at-me clothes at all. Her style was actually more along the lines of, "I made this from a bath mat/lampshade/curtain/dog bed because I wanted to, and I don't give a crap what anyone else thinks."

Even though I've personally got no interest in wearing anything other than jeans and a sweatshirt, I kind of admire that. Most people who look ridiculous just look ridiculous. With Marina there was something else going on.

"So you're Caliban," she said, depositing her sewing on a rickety stool and standing to greet me.

"Yes."

"The monster."

"That's me."

She let out a hesitant laugh and said, "We're taking a period approach for the other characters, but for you we need something different."

I nodded, as if I understood what she was talking about.

"I've sketched out a few ideas. What do you think of this?"

She opened up a notebook and showed me a drawing of a muscle-bound man with yellowy-green skin squatting on the ground, mugging angrily. He was wearing what looked like a tiny pair of leather Speedos. And nothing else.

"What's that?" I asked.

"It's you."

You know the noise people make when a chunk of food has gotten stuck in their throat so they can't speak, and they're struggling to attract the attention of someone to slap them on the back and save their life? That noise was my response.

"What do you think?" she said, smiling tentatively.

"Isn't it a bit . . . revealing? And I don't look anything like that. I'm kind of weedy."

"No you're not. Anyway, that's just a sketch. I was trying to make it look exciting."

"Couldn't I have something a bit more . . ." My voice trailed away. It was important that I found a way to communicate my abject horror at the thought of appearing in public wearing anything even vaguely resembling the garment Marina had drawn, but I had to do this without hurting her feelings or making her hate me.

"More what?"

"A bit less . . ."

"Less what?"

"Skimpy. Exposing."

"Exposing?"

"Can't you cover me up a bit more?"

"You're supposed to look wild. I could make you hairier, if you want. Glue something on to you. Would that help?"

"I don't know. I really don't know. Sorry."

"It's okay."

"I'm just . . . I'm kind of . . ."

I must have been pulling a strange expression, because when I looked at Marina her brow was suddenly furrowed with concern.

"Are you all right?" she asked.

I nodded.

"Why don't you sit down," she offered. "NOT THERE!" But it was too late. I was already on the stool. With a needle in my ass.

I stood again, handed the sewing to her, and, resisting the overpowering urge to find out if my buttock was bleeding, took the chair.

"What's the problem?" she said.

Something about her—perhaps it was the kind lilt of her voice, or maybe the sincerity in her eyes—cracked open the shell of pride I had been hiding under. A sudden, unexpected urge to tell the truth welled up in me. I felt as if I couldn't hold back any longer, but I had no idea how to express it either.

"You look miserable," she said, positioning the stool right in front of me and sitting down. "What's wrong?"

"Oh, I don't know. I just think this whole thing has been a huge mistake. I'm going to make an idiot of myself. I'm no good."

"Don't think that! There's huge competition for parts. You'd never have gotten in if you weren't talented."

"I was good in the audition. That's how I got in. Now I'm garbage."

"Why? What's changed?"

"I just can't do it. I feel self-conscious. I find it embarrassing. I can't let go of myself and actually act."

"Why not?"

"Because I'm no good. Because I know people will laugh at me for being crap."

"What was different in the audition?"

"I don't know. There was just a moment when I didn't care, and that made everything different."

"Why did you stop caring?"

"I just . . . kind of . . . lost myself in what I was doing, but I can't get that feeling back."

Marina stared at me, scrutinizing my face and then my body, her forehead furrowed in concentration.

"Sorry," I said, when the intensity of her gaze began to feel too awkward. "I don't know why I'm moaning on about this."

She looked up, her eyes suddenly bright with excitement. "I think I can help you," she said.

"How?"

"Sounds like you want a costume that helps you stop feeling like you."

"How can a costume do that?"

"That's exactly what a costume's supposed to do. How about a mask?"

"A mask?"

"Yes. You're supposed to be a monster, so it makes sense. Half-face. Over your eyes and nose and the top of your head. I can see it now. Your mouth will be free, but you'll be covered up. Do you think that would help?"

"Maybe it would."

"You won't look like you at all. And you won't feel like you. You'll feel hidden."

Marina was already sketching, muttering to herself about boils and weeping sores. I sat in silence and watched as a magnificently hideous face-covering took shape in her sketchbook.

"It's very rough," she said eventually, reaching for a pair of scissors and cutting out the drawing, "but how about something like this?"

I walked to the full-length mirror that dominated the middle of the room and placed the template over my face. I looked truly revolting.

"What do you think?" she said.

I turned to face her, curled my spine into a stoop, and extended a crooked finger in her direction. "*As wicked dew as e'er my mother brush'd with raven's feather from unwholesome fen drop on you both!"* I said. *"A south-west blow on ye and blister you all o'er! All the charms of Sycorax, toads, beetles, bats, light on you! For I am all the subjects that you have, which first was mine own king."*

Marina smiled at me nervously. "You like it then?" she asked.

Still caught up on a wave of liberating unselfconsciousness, I dropped the mask from my face, leaped across the room, and pulled her into a hug. "You're a genius!" I said. "A genius."

It was a lovely moment—but only a moment—because after approximately a second we suddenly realized that we were hugging, and how weird that was.

We both took a simultaneous step back, which in my case involved falling into a rack of Elizabethan robes. This did a handy job of dispelling the awkwardness, though at some cost to my pride.

"So do you think I could have this for rehearsals?" I asked. "Stuck on a bit of cardboard or something. While you're making the real one."

"Okay. If you think it will help."

"It's the answer. I know it is. Thank you so much."

"It's nothing."

"It's not nothing. It's everything."

Suddenly the tension was back, as I realized for the first

time that although Jennifer had, on occasion, looked toward me and made eye contact, Marina actually looked *at* me, and into me. It suddenly struck me that even though she wore insane clothes and had wonky hair, and wasn't what you'd call pretty, something in Marina's eyes made her strangely beautiful. Not fashion-model beautiful, or movie-star beautiful, or even Jennifer beautiful, but beautiful to me.

OPTIMISTIC BRAIN: *This girl has the most alive and intelligent and heartbreakingly empathetic eyes. She's stunning.*
PESSIMISTIC BRAIN: *She'll never want you, you loser.*
DICK: *PHHWOOOAAAAARRRRRGGGHHHH! Kiss her! Smooch her! Smooch her now! With tongues!*
OPTIMISTIC BRAIN: *We need to establish a friendship first.*
PESSIMISTIC BRAIN: *Why would she want to be friends with us? You're dreaming.*
DICK: *Kiss her now! Now! She wants you!*
PESSIMISTIC BRAIN: *You mean* you *want* her. *There's a difference.*
DICK: *You're so boring. You think too much.*
PESSIMISTIC BRAIN: *I'm a brain. That's my job.*
DICK: *I can think too!*
PESSIMISTIC BRAIN: *You only ever have one thought. That's not thinking.*

DICK: Yes it is.
PESSIMISTIC BRAIN: No it isn't.
DICK: Yes it is.

While I conducted this delicately poised internal debate, a silence stretched between us, during which it seemed wrong to look away, and equally wrong to continue staring at her.

"I should go," I said, when the quiet began to feel like a rubber band on the brink of snapping. "I have to be at . . . I'm expected at . . . a place. Home, in fact. Where I live. I have to get home."

"Okay."

"Okay."

"I'll talk to Mr. Duverne, and if he's happy with the mask idea I'll get you back for a fitting."

"Okay. I'll talk to him too."

"Okay."

"Okay."

"Okay."

It was obvious by this point that we had exchanged an excessive number of okays, but the cycle now felt strangely hard to break.

"Okay," I said, one last time, and hurried from the room, returning briefly to give back the Elizabethan ruff that had somehow attached itself to my ankle.

As I walked home, Big Thoughts swished and thumped around my skull like dirty sneakers in a washing machine:

- *Was it possible to love two women at once?*
- *Was "love" the right word for liking someone who already had a boyfriend and clearly thought of me as a total nobody?*
- *Had that been a* moment *with Marina?*
- *Maybe it had!*
- *Did the yet-to-be-appropriately-named sensation I felt toward Marina alter the status of my similar-but-equally-inexplicable feelings for Jennifer, with whom I'd never come even close to having a moment?*
- *Did any of this matter when I was surely destined to remain a virgin until I was thirty?*
- *Since my dad started to go bald at thirty-five, and nobody thinks bald men are hot, would I have to cram a whole lifetime of sex into five years?*
- *Why was everything so complicated?*
- *Why was love so painful?*
- *Oh, woe; oh, woe; oh, woe!*

The sexting fail rebound illusion

The first full run-through was scheduled to take place on a Saturday morning. The buildup was intense, with a buzz spreading through the cast as we began to see the play grow from a collection of fragments rehearsed in small rooms to a complete story performed by a cohesive group. My performance had improved hugely since Marina gave me a cardboard mask to rehearse in, and I was surprised to find myself looking forward to the run-through as an opportunity to show everyone that I was no longer the theatrical equivalent of dog vomit.

This was the first time I'd ever not dreaded a rehearsal, but my newfound confidence was immediately shaken up when Jennifer walked in, twenty minutes late, in floods of tears. It may have simply been because I was sitting nearest to the door, but the first thing she did (after making sure everyone had noticed she was crying) was to fall into my arms and sob on my shoulder.

I had spent many idle hours dreaming about Jennifer flinging herself at me, and now it was finally happening, but not in the manner of my fantasies. This was a far noisier, snottier, more unsettling experience.

While Mr. Duverne gave a long speech about acoustics and projection, Jennifer lifted her head from my shoulder, noisily blew her nose and whisper-sobbed into my ear, "I've left him."

"Felipe?"

"Yes."

It's a confusing sensation when your feelings of sympathy and concern for an unhappy friend coincide with a desire to leap up and dance for joy. Employing all my restraint and tact, I forcefully held back any expression of the jig-dancing that was occupying nine-tenths of my brain.

"Really? When?" I asked, putting my hand over my mouth in what I hoped would look like a gesture of surprise, when in fact I needed the pressure of a finger and thumb to pry the corners of my mouth out of a smile.

"Last night. He sexted me."

"And that made you dump him?"

"He sexted me with the wrong name!"

"Which name? Is that bad?"

"He's cheating on me! He's sexting other girls!"

"Right. Wow. What a bastard!"

I had a rough idea what sexting was but no idea how you actually did it. I decided to contain my curiosity though. This didn't feel like the right moment to ask for a how-to guide.

"I thought he'd apologize and come crawling back," she sobbed.

"And?"

"Nothing. He says monogamy suffocates him and he won't be put in a box."

"He has a thing about boxes. He said the same thing to me about being a loser."

"He's a pig! I hate him!"

"I always had a feeling he was going to hurt you. That's why maybe you thought I was staring during rehearsals. Which I wasn't. But if it seemed like I was, it must have been because I was worried about you. Concerned. As a friend."

"I thought I loved him. I thought he loved me."

"He loves himself, and that's it. He'd never give you what you deserve. You're too good for him." I had no idea where these phrases were coming from, or what they even actually meant. I just heard them come out of my mouth, presumably regurgitated from some TV show that had lodged itself in my subconscious without ever stopping off in any accessible part of my memory.

Jennifer looked at me with her tear-filled eyes, and my Trouser Tent Early Warning Alarm went off.

"Do you really think so?" she asked, turning toward me, causing our knees to touch.

HONK! HONK! THREAT LEVEL RISING TO AMBER! HONK! HONK!

"Yes! You should be with a guy who respects you for who you are."

"Oh, you're so sweet," she said, giving my forearm a brief stroke.

"I just . . . hate to see you so down," I replied, momentarily patting the back of her hand.

HONK! HONK! WE HAVE LIFTOFF! EVACUATE THE AREA! EVACUATE THE AREA!

"Thanks, Sam. You're a true friend."

"I'm here for you. Whenever you need."

The situation was now perfectly primed for me to offer a friendly, comforting hug, but the alarm signals I was receiving from below—*REVERSE! TROUSER TENT AT CRITICAL! REVERSE! CLEAR THE CONTACT ZONE!*—made this maneuver far too risky.

I then became dimly aware that Mr. Duverne was

shouting at us for not listening, but I didn't really hear what he said because I wasn't listening.

When the cast had to stand in a circle for a warm-up game, Jennifer held my hand pointedly, staring all the while at Felipe, who put such effort into pretending not to notice what she was doing that it was completely obvious how much he noticed. This was a great feeling, almost as enjoyable as watching Felipe and Jennifer attempting to do their love scenes now that they couldn't stand the sight of each other. These dialogues, which until recently had suffered from a distracting excess of sexual chemistry—I don't think Shakespeare intended the characters to look at one another as if they were nanoseconds away from going carnal—had suddenly gone the other way. Their passionate declarations of love were so lifeless they sounded almost sarcastic. Suddenly, my Caliban was no longer the weak point in the play.

I did feel bad seeing Jennifer gradually lose confidence in her performance, but watching Felipe flounder onstage was deeply satisfying. I felt as if I could see him discovering the concept of self-doubt and responding with the disbelief and amazement of a kitten trying to figure out snow.

Quite aside from the Jennifer/Felipe meltdown, I sensed my position as cast laughingstock evaporate as the run-through progressed. Performing in a cardboard mock-up of the planned mask, I felt as if the real me was hidden away, liberating a new unselfconscious version of myself to act the part. When I was onstage, the auditorium seemed quieter, the onlookers stiller than before. People were actually watching and listening, rather than whispering comments and chuckling, and the more I sensed this stillness and attention, the more confident I felt. Toward the end, it dawned on me that I was actually enjoying myself.

Immediately after the final scene Marina rushed up from the auditorium, where she'd been taking notes, and leaped toward me, taking both my hands in hers.

"You were amazing!" she said.

"Really?"

"Really!"

"I feel completely different wearing the mask."

"I knew you would! The finished version's almost ready. And I've got some more ideas. Will you come on Monday after school for a fitting?"

"Sure. I won't have to wear leather Speedos, will I?"

"I've thought of something else. It's a sort of fur onesie. But cool."

"*A fur onesie?*"

"Not real fur!"

"It's the onesie thing I'm worried about."

"You'll like it. You're going to look amazing."

As Marina hurried away to confer with other cast members about their costumes, a stream of people congratulated me on my performance. Even Ulf, who had never before said anything to me other than to point out what I was doing wrong, patted my arm, gave me a long, ice-blue Nordic stare, and said, "Nice."

This was as effusive as Ulf ever got about anything, and I was momentarily choked up with gratitude at this Scandinavian-style gush of unqualified praise.

"Thanks," I said.

He nodded and walked away, looking slightly wearied by the length of our conversation.

Whether people were genuinely impressed by my acting or just relieved that I was no longer single-handedly ruining the play, I wasn't entirely sure, but it didn't seem to matter.

When I looked around the auditorium for Jennifer, wondering what she might say about my transformed performance, I couldn't spot her. I searched the backstage area, pretending to be looking for a lost prop, but she'd vanished.

Only as I was setting off for home did I come across her, sitting on a wall in the parking lot. Her shoulders were slumped, and her face was hidden behind a raised hand. She didn't even look up as I approached.

"Are you okay?" I asked.

She lifted her chin slowly, and I saw on her features not melodramatic misery or attention-seeking angst but a pallor of genuine despair. Her eyes were red and puffy, as if she'd been crying again.

I looked around to see if there was anyone nearby better equipped to deal with this situation—and literally *anyone* else would have been—but nobody was in sight.

"I don't know what to do," she said. "I was useless."

I sat down next to her, contemplated patting her on the back, decided against it, and said, "No, you weren't. It was . . . you were . . ."

"The whole thing was a total embarrassment."

"You just had a bad day."

"It was a disaster, and the dress rehearsal's next week."

"Today was just a blip. It doesn't mean anything."

"You don't know how hard it is to do those scenes with Felipe, after what's happened between us."

"Forget him. That's in the past."

"But doing love scenes with him! It's impossible!"

"It'll be easier next time. You're an amazing actor . . . actress . . . actor. Everyone says so."

"Really?"

A glimmer of hope seemed to flash across her face, and it occurred to me that perhaps I wasn't as appalling at consoling a female as I'd assumed I would be. "Yes! Of course!" I said, warming to my newfound Dear Abby persona. "And if you do those scenes exactly how you did them before you broke up, it'll show him that you've moved on. That he means nothing to you."

"You think?"

"I know you can do it. You're going to be amazing."

She gave a reluctant smile and our eyes locked. "You're a good listener," she said, after what felt like a meaningful pause.

"Well, I—'

"It's unusual," she interrupted. "You're different from other guys."

My pulse started hammering, and my breathing suddenly became shallow and fast. Due to some strange glitch in the evolutionary process, when my body perceives even the faintest glimmer of a possibility of romantic activity, it responds as if a grizzly bear has jumped out from behind a nearby bush. I have no idea if this happens to other people, but I suspect not.

"You're very sensitive," she added, holding my gaze.

Sensitive! Nobody had *ever* said that to me before.

This was definitely it. Not just a moment, but *the* moment. The one I had dreamed of. The high point of my life so far. The culmination of everything of any value I had ever undertaken at any point since the moment of my birth. Finally! At long last! A girl liked me!

"I have sensitive teeth," I said, for LITERALLY NO REASON WHATSOEVER. Just blind panic. Total loss of blood supply to the brain. "No . . . I just mean . . . it's good to . . . you know . . . listen," I added, flailing for any fragments of language I could find that might string themselves into something resembling a sentence.

She smiled at me, pretending not to notice that I had suddenly become an utter moron, and I realized there was now only one thing to do. The conversation had ended, but neither of us was doing the things you do at the end of a conversation. We were just sitting there, staring at each other. I'd seen this scenario in films, countless times. The next step was clear.

I slowly began to lean toward her, and was already puckering my lips in readiness for an attempted kiss when she said, "Or do you think maybe I should take him back?"

I leaned back. I unpuckered. My heart sank into my rectum and sat there giving off feeble, pukey throbs.

"What?" I said, when the capacity for speech eventually returned.

"For the sake of the play."

"I don't understand."

"This is my big opportunity. I've waited years to get

a part like this, and there's an agent coming on the opening night. I can't screw it up."

"Yes, but . . ."

"Those love scenes used to be great. We clicked. It was so real."

"Yes, but you can't . . . I mean . . ."

"I won't get another opportunity like this."

"Of course you will."

"Not if I mess it up."

"I thought you hated him."

"I do."

"So you can't take him back!"

"I also still love him."

"Do you?"

"I don't know. But I could act as if I did."

"That's crazy!"

"No, it isn't. If I want to be an actor, I have to *be* an actor."

"Only onstage."

"No! It's a way of life! It has to be who you are."

"But when you're not acting you have to be real."

"Acting *is* real. They're not opposites."

"Are you saying . . . ?"

"Sam—you're amazing!"

"Am I?"

"Ten minutes ago I was in total despair. You've shown me a way forward."

"Have I?"

"I'm going to call him."

"Felipe?"

"Yeah. I'm not going to make it too easy, but I'll let him know if he plays his cards right . . ."

"You'll take him back?"

"It's the only thing to do! For the good of the play. I'd be letting down the whole cast if I didn't."

"But . . ."

"You're such a great friend, Sam. I can talk to you about anything. Thank you so much," she said, sliding off the wall and giving me a peck on the cheek.

With a toss of her hair, she swept away toward the curb. Francine's vast car pulled up, and a window slid down as Jennifer climbed in. "How did it go? Was it *wonderful*? Do you want a lift?" said Francine.

I shook my head.

"Okay. Give your mom a kiss from me," she trilled, and with the muted roar of perfectly tuned German engineering, the vehicle accelerated away, Francine waving theatrically, Jennifer, head down, no doubt already messaging warped mind games to Felipe.

Four terrifying words

I walked slowly home, snuck into the house, and trudged straight to my bedroom without even stopping for a snack. I couldn't face talking to anyone. My heart still felt as if it was lodged in the depths of my lower intestine. My body was clenched into a knot of embarrassment, regret, confusion, and disappointment, and I had the sensation that if I relaxed, my heart would fall out of my asshole and die on the carpet like a beached jellyfish.

After a while, my phone beeped with a message: "*It's all good. Problem solved! Thanks for being there for me. J xxx.*"

I didn't reply. There was nothing to say, other than perhaps "*Why is the universe so cruel?*", which I decided might strike the wrong note.

I set my phone to Silent (for a moment I even contemplated actually *switching it off*) and decided that I would spend the next twenty-four hours lying on my bed with the curtains drawn. There was simply no other option. I couldn't move, and I couldn't speak.

Then Mom called up the stairs that dinner was ready, and I realized I was starving, so I went down to eat, but I knew it was highly unlikely that I would be engaging in any conversation.

Freya was in one of her chatty moods, so for the entire duration of the main course nobody even noticed that I wasn't speaking. After the plates were cleared away, Mom disappeared to fetch something we all assumed was going to be a dessert.

How wrong we were. She returned holding a piece of paper.

This was ominous.

Mom sat and placed the paper in front of her, just as she would have done if it had been, say, an apple crumble. Oh, if only it had been an apple crumble!

An edgy hush filled the room. Mom then uttered the four words everyone in the family most feared.

"I've written a poem," she said.

There was a long silence.

"Would you like to hear it?"

There was another, even longer, silence. It had been a strange day of many highs and lows. This was a new low.

"Okay," she continued, lifting the paper from the table. "This is something I workshopped with my group."

"Something you workshopped?" said Ethan.

"Yes," said Mom.

"At your workshop?"

"Yes, actually."

"The workshop in your workshop?"

"Where are you going with this?" asked Mom frostily.

"Nowhere. I'm just asking. Workshopping my vocabulary."

"Why do you always have to give me . . ." Mom stopped herself and took a slow, deep breath.

"Were you about to say 'crap'?" asked Freya.

"'Guff,'" said Mom.

"You can say 'crap,'" said Freya. "Everyone else says 'crap.'"

"Not me."

"Yes you do. I've heard you," said Freya.

"Can I just read the poem?"

There was another silence, even longer than the previous two.

"Okay," she said. "This is a short piece called 'Menopause: Me, No Pause.' I want to share it with you because I've been discussing with my group how important it is for young people to grow up in a house without body shaming, ageism, or repression. If this makes any of you uncomfortable, just go with it. Nature is beautiful."

The urge to run away was overwhelming, but for some reason I couldn't get up. The kind of paralysis that freezes shell-shocked soldiers on the battlefield had taken over my body.

Mom tapped her sheet of paper against the tabletop, and in a low, swooping voice began to read aloud.

My body:
Sacred,
Pure,
Alive.

Like the moon
Month by month
I fill and empty with the fluid of life,
Fluid of death,
Womb tomb home.

A private everywhere, a universe inside me,
My wellspring,
My fecund earth,
Fertile,
Sacred,
Pure,
Alive.

Month by month
Year by year
I empty and fill
Until now,
Ripe with age,
I am spent.

My children blossom into adulthood.
Their own fecundity ripening by the day,
While I recede
Like a tide
Drifting out
Smoothing the sand of yesterday,
The sands of yesteryear.

I am less; I am more.
Stately,
Proud,
Retreating as I advance into new selves,
Fresh oceans of creativity.

I am.
I feel.
I make.

Yesterday, today, and tomorrow.
Forever me, no pause.

She laid her paper flat on the table and looked at us all, one by one. Nobody spoke. Nobody could even make eye contact. I thought I might actually rather die than have to acknowledge that the last three minutes of my life had happened. There was no excuse for making your children listen to that. The words "fecundity" and "ripening" simply have no place at a family dinner table.

"You don't have to say anything," she said eventually. "It's a very personal poem. Just let it soak in."

"Can we go now?" said Ethan.

As poetry criticism goes, this struck me as spot-on.

"I think I've found my medium," muttered Mom, seemingly talking to herself.

In situations like this, anything other than a "no" counts as a "yes." Ethan and I immediately sprinted upstairs and threw ourselves into my bedroom.

"That was beyond weird," I said.

"We have to wipe that from our memories," he replied. "Don't mention it ever again. Okay?"

"Okay. And if she writes another poem . . . ?"

"We run," he said. "We just run. Heads down. Run. Run away. It's Dad's problem. He can deal with it."

"What if she tries to make us stay?"

"We keep running. I'll do the dishes, I'll tidy my room, I'll even mow the lawn, but listening to Mom's poetry is above and beyond. That's not part of the deal."

We discussed poetry-avoidance strategies for a while longer, debating whether a fake epileptic seizure would be enough to divert her from a threatened reading; then I told Ethan that things were going a little better with the school play. He seemed pleased by this news, while also giving the impression of not being remotely interested, but this was still a significant improvement on ignoring me all the time, which was until recently his usual approach.

I was on the verge of asking his advice on my Jennifer-heartbreak situation but couldn't quite get over the embarrassment of admitting that I'd been deluded enough to think someone like her might possibly be interested in me. Ethan then launched into an update on his supposedly-gay-band-riven-with-forbidden-heterosexual-lust scenario. There was only a week to go before their showcase in front of Darius's dad's music industry friends, and Cass had managed to rein in Veronika-the-drummer's band-imploding jealous tantrums by convincing her that she felt nothing for Ethan. This had resulted in a strange pattern of stolen glances and momentary brushes of fleeting physical contact between him and Cass, which, according to Ethan, was so erotic that he was in a permanent condition of thinking his balls might explode.

"Okay—you've inherited the Too Much Information gene," I said. "That's enough."

"It's crazy," he continued. "Holding back is even hotter than moving forward. I just think about her all the time. And the way she looks at me, I know she's thinking the same thing."

"How do you know?"

"I can feel it. It's like an electricity."

"Except you can't switch it off."

"Exactly."

"Or use it to power household gadgets."

"No."

"So how is it like electricity?"

"Okay—it's more like radio waves. Some kind of secret signal that nobody else can see."

This was valuable information for avoiding another school-parking-lot-style wipeout.

"So if I send a girl I-like-you signals and she looks back in roughly the same way, does that mean she's interested?" I asked.

"Usually. But it all depends how good you are at giving the look and knowing when you're getting it back."

"How do you recognize it?"

"You just do."

"But how do you *know*?"

"If you're definitely *not* getting the look, then it's not the look. If you think it might be, it probably is. Unless she just likes you as a friend, in which case it isn't."

"HOW ARE YOU SUPPOSED TO TELL THE DIFFERENCE!?"

"Take it easy! What's up with you?"

"Nothing."

"Who's the girl?"

"What girl?"

"The girl who's turning you into a psycho."

"What are you talking about?"

"Who is it?"

"Nobody."

"Tell me."

"I don't have a girlfriend! I just . . . thought I came close the other day, with this girl I've liked for ages, then I made a total idiot of myself by kind of sort of making a move, but doing it so badly I don't know if she even noticed. Then there's also this other girl, who's more like a friend-type person, but even though I always thought she was the one I didn't like, now she's the one I can't stop thinking about, so I think the one I thought I didn't like is actually the one I do like, especially since the one I always thought I did like turns out to be a total nightmare—even though I do still kind of like her a bit, without actually wanting to—but because I used to think I didn't like the one who I've realized I actually do like, she probably thinks I still don't, even though I definitely do, and now I don't know if we're in a friends-type place or a something-else place. You know what I mean?"

"No. I have no idea what you just said."

"It's complicated and it doesn't make any sense and I have no idea what to do, but I can't think about anything else, and it's driving me crazy!"

"I can see that," he said, raising one eyebrow.

"I thought this whole thing was supposed to be fun, but actually it's agony!"

"I know. It's better than just giving up and being a virgin all your life though, isn't it?"

"That might still happen."

"Hah!" said Ethan, standing up and drifting out of the room, which was how most conversations with my brother ended, as if I was a TV he could switch off as soon as he'd had enough. Mind you, that was better than being a TV he never wanted to switch on in the first place.

The flattened roadkill of my self-esteem

Monday was the day of my mask-fitting with Marina. This wasn't going to require anything more of me than standing still while ensuring my head didn't change size—not much of a challenge, really—but the further I got through the day, the more anxious I became. The problem was, I both did and didn't want to be alone with Marina. After the disaster in the school parking lot with Jennifer, I had lost all confidence in my ability to recognize the friendship/flirting boundaries, and I felt certain that if one of our awkward moments happened I was bound to respond in the wrong way and screw the whole thing up. Equally, if there were no awkward moments, then I'd know that I'd already screwed the whole thing up. I desperately wanted to communicate how I felt about her, but I had no idea how to do this. I just knew that if I tried it would go wrong.

When the end of the school day arrived, and I found myself heading for Marina's private lair, I felt like someone walking into a physics exam without ever having attended a physics class. I decided the best way to mask my confusion, fear, and incompetence was with a display of George Clooneyesque self-assurance, which, if carried off with enough conviction, might even somehow convince myself.

The first challenge to this strategy came with the sight of her closed door. Knock or barge in? Loud, confident, manly knock or quiet, modest, understated knock? Or just a casual knock-and-enter without waiting for a reply? I considered these options for a while, until, by some embarrassing coincidence, Marina opened the door and found me standing there, gazing blankly at the door handle, looking as unlike George Clooney as it is possible to be without wearing a blond wig and a miniskirt.

"You're here?" she said.

"Yeah, I was just wondering . . . I mean . . . I just arrived . . . I mean I thought I was a bit early and I didn't want to intrude so I . . . I mean, yeah. I'm here. That's what I am. Here."

"Great. Come in," she said, with a slight curl at the corners of her mouth which looked suspiciously like a suppressed smirk.

"I brought my head."

"Excellent. So let's try this bad boy on. I hope you like it."

She opened a box and removed a lurid papier-mâché mask, which was at the same time one of the most beautiful and ugliest things I had ever seen. The skin was a reddish yellow, covered in boils and warts, with a hideous snub nose and a bald scalp dotted with patchy tufts of greasy hair.

"Wow!" I said. "That is revolting! I love it!"

"Do you really?"

Hearing the doubt in her voice, I realized she was nervous too. Not as nervous as me, obviously—she wasn't a freak—but genuinely concerned that I wouldn't like the mask.

"Yes! Totally!" I said. "How long did it take?"

"Hours. Days. It's taken me forever," she said, with a sighing half laugh that somehow expressed both relief at having finished and a hint of pride in what she had made.

"It's incredible! Really."

"Do you want to try it on?"

"Can't wait."

She slipped it over my head, attaching it in place with a pair of Velcro strips. Three-quarters of my face was hidden, with only my mouth, chin, and one cheek uncovered. As soon as the mask was on, I felt transformed, taken over by an urge to stoop and limp and yell curses. I turned to the mirror and saw an extraordinary, repulsive, otherworldly beast. Sam, the teenage boy who still wished he lived in Stevenage, had disappeared.

"Do you want to put on the rest of the costume?" Marina asked. "It's behind there."

She pointed at a wooden folding screen, and I slipped behind it to see what she had made. Draped over a chair was a mangy fur leotard, caked in smears of ingrained filth and dotted with clusters of weeping boils. I stripped to my underwear, wriggled into it, and pounced out from behind the screen. The words that tumbled from my mouth at this point weren't particularly Shakespearean:

Sexy sexy ooh, yeah!
I'm so sexy!
I'm so sexy!

For no particular reason, I chose to accompany this improvised song with a kind of disco-king prance across the room.

This was very much not part of the Clooney Strategy, but what with the fur leotard and boil-covered monster head, that plan had already been comprehensively abandoned in favor of a more freewheeling dick-around-like-an-overexcited-kid-and-hope-for-the-best approach. This wasn't so much a strategy as just what happens when you *are* an overexcited kid and you forget that you're supposed to be hiding it.

By the time I finished my dance, I saw that Marina was laughing hysterically, though whether she was laughing with me or at me I wasn't quite sure.

"I also made you these," she said, handing me a couple of short sticks, like tiny crutches. "I thought maybe you could use them to stoop and give you a kind of spidery walk. Only if you want. It's just an idea."

I took the sticks and tried out her suggestion, clattering to and fro around the room like a trapped insect.

"This is cool," I said.

"Give me one of your lines."

I approached Marina, gave a mournful grunt, then spoke in a voice I'd never found before: deep, slightly lisping but laden with wounded melancholy:

Be not afeard. The isle is full of noises,
Sounds and sweet airs, that give delight and hurt not.
Sometimes a thousand twangling instruments
Will hum about mine ears, and sometime voices
That, if I then had waked after long sleep,
Will make me sleep again. And then, in dreaming,
The clouds methought would open and show riches

Ready to drop upon me, that when I waked,
I cried to dream again.

I looked up at her through my hideous mask, and our eyes locked. I held her gaze for longer than I'd ever stared into another person's eyes.

"That was beautiful," she said, flushing slightly, then rapidly looking away as if panicked that she'd said something inappropriate, then glancing back to see if her panic was justified.

"Thanks," I said. "It's the only point in the whole play when he reveals his gentle side and dares to show what's really in his heart."

A moment of stillness and hush settled over us. The sound of a distant playground yelp drifted into the room. I thought about what I'd just said, and though I had no idea where those words came from, I suddenly realized that quite by accident I had Clooneyed! What a line!

Marina looked at me, smiled, and said nothing. The space between us seemed to shrink, and also somehow pulsate with a mysterious, vibrant energy.

This was it! The secret radio waves Ethan had been talking about! We were having a moment! This wasn't a humiliating-misunderstanding pseudo-moment, like in the parking lot with Jennifer, but a real one. With a girl I actually liked!

Marina and I were staring at each other, in tense-but-not-awkward silence, and I knew she was thinking what I was thinking.

At least I thought I knew.

But I also knew that everything I knew was wrong.

Was she thinking what I was thinking?

I thought so.

But what did *I* know?

Nothing.

Was this *really* a moment?

Or was I just overthinking?

Or underthinking?

Did that even actually mean anything, or was I now just standing there making up words when it was perfectly obvious that I ought to be DOING SOMETHING?

But what was it I should be doing?

Making a move, *obviously*.

It was time. All the required elements were in place. Nothing further needed to be said. I just had to kiss her. On the face. Ideally in the vicinity of her mouth.

Unfortunately, I was wearing a boil-and-wart-covered mask, and any attempt at lip-to-lip contact was likely to result in impaling one of Marina's eyeballs on my papier-mâché nose.

I tried to reach around for the Velcro to release myself

from the mask, but realized that my fur leotard was too tight around the armpits. I suspect this is not a problem that has often messed up George Clooney's romantic maneuvers.

"I'll help you," said Marina, stepping behind me and pulling open the straps. With each *rrrrrrip* of released Velcro, the pitch of sexual tension in the room went down a notch. By the time my face was free of the mask, the moment was no longer a moment. We were just two people standing in a room, one with a curiously sweaty top three-quarters of a face.

"So how did it feel?" said Marina.

"You mean . . . the mask?"

"Yeah."

"Great," I said. "Thank you. It's going to change everything."

"I hope so. Not that you weren't good before. I just mean, I hope it helps."

"It will."

The room now seemed to fill with what can only be called an anti-moment. A kind of deflated, anticlimactic, something-almost-happened-then-didn't-so-maybe-even-thinking-about-it-was-a-huge-stupid-mistake sensation.

"Do you need it adjusted at all?" she asked.

For a second I thought she might be referring to

my personality, but then I realized she was talking about my costume.

"The armpits are a bit tight," I said, which did little to restore the romantic vibe in the room.

"Okay," she said. "That's easily fixed. I had Jennifer in here earlier and you wouldn't believe how many alterations she asked for."

"I would, actually."

"After all those tears at the run-through, it turns out she and Felipe are back together again."

"Yeah, she told me," I said.

"You and her are very chummy, aren't you?"

"Not really. She kind of blows hot and cold."

"Not with me," said Marina. "I get cold and cold."

"She's a strange person. You can't really take what she says at face value."

"You mean, she's a liar."

"Well—she's an actress," I said.

"Acting when you're not acting is called lying. She's a fake. She'll do anything to get what she wants."

"I know."

"Jennifer and Felipe deserve each other, if you ask me," said Marina. "Not that I'm bitchy or anything. I just can't stand them. I've deliberately made Felipe's pants give him a massive wedgie, just because he was so rude to me in the fitting. I know that's immature, but I couldn't help it."

"Brilliant. That is so good."

"Honestly, the pants go so far up his crack they're going to make his eyes water. It's like dental floss, but for a bum."

"I love you!"

"What?"

"I love it. I mean, I love it. What you did. It. I love *it*."

"Okay."

Suddenly those radio waves were crackling between us again, and this time I wasn't covered in papier-mâché warts.

I took a deep breath.

"Listen," I said, "I know you're really busy with costumes for the play and everything, and even after it's finished you're probably going to be busy with other stuff, so there probably isn't time or anything, but if there's an evening when you're free—I mean, I know there probably won't be or anything—not for ages—but if there is, do you think maybe you and me could maybe go to a movie? Maybe. Or something."

"Okay."

YEEEEEEESSSSSSSSSSSSSSSSSSSSSSSSSSSSSSSS SSSSSSSSS! YEEEEEEEEEEEEEEEEEAAAAAAA

AAAAAAAHHHHHHHHHHHHHHHHH! OHHHH
YESSSITY YES YES! WHAT A MAN! SLAM DUNK!
HOME RUN! WHAM BAM KERRCHING!

"But only if you wear the mask."

"Really?"

Only when Marina almost collapsed on the floor with laughter did I realize that the mask comment had been a joke, but not a joke nearly so funny, apparently, as me, in a moment of confusion, believing her.

With each passing cascade of laughs I felt a shade less triumphant. Eventually she recovered and squeezed my arm affectionately. "You're so funny," she said.

Whether this was a compliment or an insult I had no idea. It may well have been both, but I decided not to ask, because in my experience once you enter the Forest of Sexual Discombobulation, it's best to retreat. Once you get lost in there, you're not getting out without making an idiot of yourself.

"I gotta scoot," I said, which is not a sentence I had ever uttered before, but this kind of vocabulary mishap is exactly what happens on the fringes of the aforementioned forest.

Before I could embarrass myself again, or give her a chance to change her mind about our movie outing, I turned and strode out of the room. I was halfway through the school, and becoming increasingly aware of the stares I appeared to be drawing, when I passed Just Call Me Tony. His greeting, "Method acting, huh?" made me realize I was still dressed in my mange-fur leotard.

"Oh, shit," I said, which in any other school would be an unwise thing to say to a teacher, but in the North London Academy for the Gifted and Talented was more or less okay, as long as you timed it right.

I turned to run back to the costume room, but Just Call Me Tony stopped me by putting his arm around my shoulders and pulling me into his cloud of vegan halitosis. "Sam, I just want to say I've been hearing great things about your acting—that you're really digging into the role."

At this point, the double doors behind us opened, signaling the end of orchestra practice. Streams of pupils poured out, all of them having to divert around me, dressed in a fur leotard, getting a hug from the teaching staff's most legendary knob. This sight drew a parade of lingering stares.

"I have to go. I forgot my—"

"Listen, it can be hard to take a compliment, and I know better than anyone that teachers in mainstream education are guilty of dishing out criticism without a counterbalance of praise. Our methodology is very different here."

"Yeah, I know . . ."

"So it's important to me to say this. Look at me, Sam. Look at me."

"I really have to . . ."

"Look at me."

Just Call Me Tony physically turned me toward him and placed a firm hand on each of my shoulders. It pained me, but I looked at him. At the edges of my vision I could see every member of the school orchestra staring wordlessly as they passed. This whole episode was doing to my ego what trucks do to squirrels.

"Sam—I want you to know that I appreciate what you've achieved here. You had a hard transition. Mainstream education is a cave, but this place is like a summer meadow. Cave dwellers get agoraphobia when they first learn how big the world is, how much freedom there really is out there that the forces of conformity don't want you to know about. Have you ever heard of Stockholm syndrome?"

"No. Yes. Er . . . I'll look it up. Thanks very much. I have to go."

I ducked, wriggled free, and ran back to the costume room in search of my clothes, dragging behind me the flattened roadkill of my self-esteem.

The last thing you would ever want to ask your mother

When Mr. Duverne saw me perform in full costume for the first time, his eyes filled with tears. This happened to him about eight times a day, so it didn't mean much, and I suspected his weeping was caused less by the moving nature of my performance than by simple relief that I was not, after all, going to irradiate his play with crapness.

He called me in for an individual movement rehearsal, where I got into costume and the pair of us charged around the drama room using Marina's little crutches, grunting, yelling, and trying different moves. By the end, I felt as if I'd unearthed some kind of inner wildness that I could channel into my portrayal of Caliban. With the mask and the costume, and now a nonhuman way of propelling myself around the stage, I'd found a way to step into a new persona. I'd never had any feeling like it: a sensation of being released from my own body and transported to a place where I could perform as if some outside force was controlling me, as if it wasn't really me up onstage.

As the cast gathered together in the dressing room during the last couple of hours before the final dress rehearsal, a buzz of anticipation built within the group that seemed to push out all petty rivalries and dislikes. Except for me and Felipe, obviously. I still thought he was a humongous prick. But even he seemed infected by the spirit of cast camaraderie, and when the ten-minute call for curtain-up came through, with us both in full costume—him as a handsome prince with a massive wedgie and me as a hideous boil-covered monster—he came over and shook my hand.

"Break a leg," he said to me, which is what actors are supposed to say to each other because it's apparently bad luck to say "good luck."

"Good luck," I replied, wondering fleetingly if this might bring him enough bad luck to actually break his leg, and whether I would feel remotely guilty if this happened.

Rapid conclusion: I wouldn't.

"Listen, bud," he went on, still not letting go of my hand. "I just want you to know that even though we've had our differences and stuff, I respect you as a performer."

"Thanks," I replied, pulling my hand free.

"I know you've always been intimidated by me—jealous even—but I think it's big of you, the way you've put that into the past. And I appreciate what you did for Jennifer."

"What I did for Jennifer?"

"Yeah. She said she was in a dark place. A really dark place. After our split."

"What, the one that lasted a day?"

"Yeah, it hit her really hard, and she said she turned to you. She said you were a rock."

"A what?"

"She feels things very deeply, and I think what you said to her about me helped turn her back to the light."

"About *you*?"

"She was lost, then she came back to me. Between us we saved her from herself."

"I didn't say anything."

"You're too modest."

"That's not a problem you struggle with, is it?"

"Listen—I just want you to know, despite what anyone else might say, you *are* invited to the cast party. Straight after closing night. At my place. A friend of mine who's almost definitely going to be signed to an indie label was going to do a live set with his band, but it turns out he's on tour at the moment, way out in South London somewhere, so it looks like it'll just be me DJing. Unless I can book another band at the last minute."

"Kanye West might be free," I said, momentarily forgetting that humor was an alien concept to Felipe.

"He's too famous," said Felipe.

"Okay. Yeah. You're right."

"There's no way I could afford him. And he lives in America, anyway."

"I wasn't thinking."

"Someone just starting out is what I'm looking for."

"Okay. I get it."

"Anyway, even without a band it'll be wild. I've sent my parents out of town. It's going to be an all-nighter. But if you're tired and you just want to go home after the play, that's not a problem. Nobody will think that makes you more of a loser or a dweeb or any of the other things people say about you."

"It's fine. I'll come."

"Cool."

The dress rehearsal went better than I would ever have dared hope. It was my first time onstage since my movement rehearsal with Mr. Duverne, and the effect was transformative. The change didn't just come from me performing better, but from a sudden realization that I had hit a groove and wasn't going to make a fool of myself. Everything I'd ever done onstage, up to this point, had been inhibited by fear. Now, suddenly, I'd lost the fear, and this changed everything.

With Felipe and Jennifer a couple again, their scenes regained the lost sexual chemistry, and for the first time the play truly came together. After weeks of rehearsal in which everything, however polished, just looked like a bunch of kids reciting lines they'd memorized, now, at last, our characters seemed three-dimensional and believable. All of us could feel it, and Mr. Duverne sent us home on a surge of enthusiasm, reminding us that tomorrow we'd be doing the show in front of an audience, for real, and that he had now done everything he could do. From here on, it was up to us.

I floated home on a cloud of euphoria, not even aware that I was walking, but the moment I stepped through the front door, I realized something was wrong. The atmosphere was heavy, hushed, and tense.

"What's up?" I asked, walking into the doom-filled kitchen.

"It's Ethan," said Mom. "Something's happened."

"I thought his showcase was this evening. Is he back already?"

"He's been back for hours."

"How come?"

"He won't say," said Dad. "He went out for the sound-check, then came home about half an hour later, went up to his room, and won't speak or come out."

"He won't even accept cookies," said Mom.

"He turned down cookies?" I said, shocked.

"Yes."

This was bad.

"You try," said Mom. "Go up there. See if he'll talk to you."

"Okay."

"Take these," she added, passing me a packet of Oreos with the solemnity of a surgical nurse handing a surgeon his scalpel.

I took the Oreos and warily climbed the stairs. By the time I got to Ethan's door, five of the cookies had somehow transported themselves into my stomach. I have no idea how.

I knocked.

"Go away," said Ethan.

"It's me," I replied. "Are you okay?"

"What do you want?"

"I've got cookies."

"I don't want cookies."

I pushed the door open. Ethan was sitting on his bed, tapping furiously at his laptop.

"Mom thinks if you don't want cookies you must be about to kill yourself. I've been sent up to check that you're still alive."

"Well, I am. But only barely."

"What's happened?"

"The showcase was a disaster. We never even got onstage."

"Why?"

"Well, you know how I said that contained passion and holding back is actually just as horny as going ahead and doing the things you want to do?"

"Kind of."

"It turns out that's not quite true."

"How do you mean?"

"Well, I got there early for the soundcheck, and so did Cass, and we were alone together for the first time in ages, and we got a bit carried away, and when Veronika arrived she walked in and we were kind of in a compromising position."

"How compromising?"

"Hands were in places where friends just don't put hands. Zips were down that really should have been up. Denial wasn't an option."

"And . . . ?"

"She freaked. Blew her top. Told us we were deceitful, manipulative, lying . . . I can't remember the rest. She just went nuts and started throwing her drum kit around, then she smashed a synth with her bare fists and disappeared. It was Darius's synth, so he went mental and told us we were a bunch of amateurs and an embarrassment, and he was quitting. So that was that. No showcase."

"Wow. That's bad."

"Yeah. We've been practicing for weeks. It was going to be our big break. Now it's all over."

"You must be gutted."

"Yeah. I reckon I'll have to go solo. I've been writing some lyrics. What do you think of this?"

Ethan looked down at the screen of his laptop and began to read aloud:

Everything is shit
Life is shit
People are shit
Everything just turns to shit

Shit shit shit
Shitty shitty shit shit
What a load of shit.

"Um . . . I like the chorus," I said.

"Do you?"

"I think it might be kind of depressing though. Could you lighten it up a bit? Maybe put in some jokes or something."

"Don't be a dick."

"Just an idea."

"I wish we could have performed *once*. After all that practice! I mean, maybe our sound wasn't ready for a showcase—maybe that's for the best—but I wish we could have at least done one gig before breaking up."

"There's no chance of some kind of . . . I don't know . . . reunion tour."

"We might be able to get Darius back, but Veronika's gone, and without a drummer we can't play. And there's nowhere to perform, anyway, so there's no point even talking about it. We're finished."

"Listen, you know Felipe? In my class? He's having a cast party after the last show on Friday and he's looking for a live band. The shitty shitty shit shit stuff might not be the right vibe, but the tunes you wrote with Cass would be cool. Everyone would love it. If you could persuade Darius . . ."

"He'd probably say yes, but without a drummer we're screwed."

"Could you use a drum machine?"

"It's not that kind of music. We need someone live. Someone kind of punky."

"Is there anyone at school?"

"Nobody. We held auditions and only three people turned up. Veronika was pretty much the only one who knew which end of a drumstick to hold."

"But if you had a drummer you'd be up for it?" I asked.

"I suppose. But we won't find someone and get them up to speed in three days. No way."

Silence fell between us as I contemplated how close we were to a solution for Ethan's disappointment. Where could we find a drummer?

Then I noticed the room was not, in fact, completely silent. A thudding sound was coming through the window from the direction of Mom's workshop/meditation space. A thudding sound that could only be described as drumming.

Doof doof hagga doof doof doof hagga doof doof badabada doof.

I looked at Ethan.

He looked at me.

"No," he said. "No way."

"Listen. She's not bad."

Doof doof hagga doof doof doof hagga doof doof badabada doof.

"No. Absolutely not. You must be joking."

Doof doof hagga doof doof doof hagga doof doof badabada doof.

"You said a band needs a thing. The gay vibe kind of backfired, so what about having a crazy mom on drums? That's a thing. Isn't it?"

"You're not serious. Please tell me you're not serious."

"She'd love it. She would so love it."

"You're insane."

"She can actually play. Listen."

Doof doof hagga doof doof doof hagga doof doof badabada doof.

"She's okay, isn't she?" said Ethan, with the dazed saucer eyes of an addict staring at the drug he craves but knows might kill him.

"I think she'd do it. I think she'd be good," I said.

"But wouldn't it make me look like an idiot?"

"Listen—I spent every single rehearsal for my play screwing everything up for the simple reason that I was afraid of looking like an idiot, then I got a costume that looks like I've draped myself in hairy vomit, and I realized it didn't matter, and that if I ran toward embarrassment as fast as I could, unafraid, and embraced it with everything I had, I'd be immune."

"Since when did you become the embarrassment guru?"

"I'm not; I just think having Mom in your band might be so uncool it's cool."

"I think I'd look like an idiot."

"But looking as if you don't care whether or not you look like an idiot is the quickest way to look cool! That's the catch!"

"I dunno."

"Do it! Ask her! You have to ask her!"

Ethan lifted himself from the bed and stared pensively out of the window toward Mom's shed. The drumming stopped, followed by what sounded like a rain-stick, chime-bar, and tambourine improvisation.

"*This* is a way to look cool?" he said.

"Possibly. It's high-risk, but . . . it might work."

"Or not."

The meaning of sick

In the last fifteen minutes before curtain-up on the opening night, something strange happened to my brain. Normally, it works at a relatively comprehensible pace, but the closer I got to having to go out onstage, the faster my thoughts seemed to whir, until they turned into some kind of nightmarish PowerPoint presentation flashing up tormenting words and phrases every half second:

HUMILIATION!

RIDICULE!

YOU'RE GOING TO FORGET YOUR LINES!

YOUR MASK IS GOING TO FALL OFF!

YOU'RE GOING TO CRAP YOURSELF IN FRONT OF FOUR HUNDRED PEOPLE!

EVERYONE IS GOING TO LAUGH AT YOU!

YOU'RE AN EGOMANIAC FOR EVEN WANT-
ING TO DO THIS!

GENUINE LUMPS OF FECES ARE GOING TO
FILL YOUR UNDERPANTS, LIVE ONSTAGE, IN
FRONT OF EVERYONE YOU KNOW.

WHY DID YOU EVEN AUDITION?

WHAT'S WRONG WITH YOU?

EVERYTHING'S WRONG WITH YOU!

BUT THE MAIN THING AT THIS MOMENT IS
YOU CAN'T ACT!

YOU'RE USELESS!

YOU'RE GOING TO LET EVERYONE ELSE
DOWN!

YOU CAN'T EVEN REMEMBER YOUR FIRST
LINE!

*WHAT'S YOUR FIRST LINE? WHAT IS IT?!
WHAT IS IT!!!???*

This soothing, meditative preshow routine was interrupted by the stage manager's call, sending performers for
the first scene up to the wings. As I was leaving the dressing
room, Marina appeared and kissed me swiftly on the lips
(tilting her head to avoid getting impaled on my papier-
mâché nose).

"It's all going to be okay," she said, staring through the
eyeholes of my mask. "You're going to be great."

The lips! Yes, the lips!

My brain/PowerPoint malfunction then spun off in an even more baffling, overwrought direction as I headed for the under-stage trapdoor through which I was due to make my first entrance. As I crouched there, waiting for my cue (*"Thou poisonous slave, got by the devil himself upon thy wicked dam, come forth!"*), I decided to try to blot out the excited/terrified noise eddying around my head by repeating my first line to myself, over and over again. This, after all, was the initial hurdle. Once I'd gotten up onstage and spoken, I'd be off. I just had to get there.

I squatted with my ear to the trapdoor, waiting, soothing myself with the comforting words, *"As wicked dew as e'er my mother brush'd with raven's feather from unwholesome fen drop on you both! As wicked dew as e'er my mother brush'd with raven's feather from unwholesome fen drop on you both! As wicked dew as e'er my mother brush'd with raven's feather from unwholesome fen drop on you both!"*

Eventually, I heard the rap of Prospero's staff on the floorboards above me, and my heart seemed to stop as the words "poisonous slave" reached my ears. For a moment, my body felt frozen where I crouched, utterly stuck, then with a surge of willpower I threw myself up through the trapdoor, monster-scampered toward my position on a polystyrene rock, and belted out my line:

As wicked dew as e'er my mother brush'd
With raven's feather from unwholesome fen
Drop on you both! A south-west blow on ye
And blister you all o'er!

At the edges of my vision I could see rows and rows of seats filled with rows and rows of heads. Over the dazzle of the footlights I could sense their hush, their attention, hundreds of eyes staring at me, but as I fixed my gaze on Prospero, who proceeded in Elizabethan English to tell me what a massive jerk I was, I felt an intoxicating sense of lift, of losing myself, of forgetting everything except my role. All fear evaporated as my focus snapped into place. I was concentrating so hard it didn't even feel as if I was concentrating at all. I lost the sense that I was acting, or remembering lines, or following rehearsed movements around the stage. Every cell of my body was pushing me onward, sucking every drop of energy I possessed into the performance, yet at the same time everything felt so natural it was almost effortless.

Offstage, between scenes, there were a few nods and smiles, but I stayed away from conversation. I held myself in the zone, wrapped up in the play, the outside world seeming to hold still and disappear, as if by some miracle this bunch of London teenagers really had transformed into princes, fools, monsters, and fairies stranded on a faraway island. The act of playing our parts in front of an attentive audience—of performance—had changed everything. In this dark space, briefly, fantasy felt more powerful than reality. This sensation was entirely new, and truly delicious.

Then, suddenly, the audience was applauding, some of them rising to their feet and whistling, and I was standing in a line with the rest of the cast, bowing. The curtain dropped, we exchanged dazed grins, and then the curtain rose again and we bowed once more, before turning to run backstage, where every one of us fell into an ecstatic group hug.

We'd pulled it off! Despite my preshow terror, I had gotten away with it. Unless everyone who congratulated me afterward was lying, I had even, against all the odds, actually been quite good.

Mr. Duverne gave a tearful (of course) speech, thanking us all for our "superhuman efforts," but for him it was relatively un-gushy. He surfed the wave of excitement and mutual congratulation only briefly before reminding us that we hadn't finished. "There are two more perform-ances," he said, "and the second night is always dangerous. There'll be less adrenaline, and to relax and think it's going to be easy is fatal. Remember, nerves are your friend.

You've done well, but now you have to go home, stay focused, and do it all again tomorrow."

This attempt to talk us down from our euphoria was greeted by a huge cheer and more hugging.

Emerging from the backstage area in my home clothes and resurfacing into the real world felt bizarre. Groups of audience members were dotted around the school auditorium, filling the space with a palpable atmosphere of parental relief. Everyone who caught my eye stared. Complete strangers turned and congratulated me on my performance.

This curious little bubble of mini-fame didn't last long, because Mom soon appeared, running toward me, which was something I hadn't seen her do since my scootering-into-traffic years. She hurled herself against my chest and swept me into a bone-crushing hug.

"You were *amazing*!" she said. "I mean, truly good. Some of the time I actually forgot it was you. I really, really am impressed. Really."

"We're very proud of you," said Dad, as I pried myself free of Mom's grip.

"I didn't understand anything anyone said or what was happening, but you were cool and I liked your mask," said Freya.

"Yeah. It was good," said Ethan. "Even you."

"You were more than good!" shrieked Mom, at an embarrassingly high volume. "You were the best! You really were."

"Mom! It's not a competition. Come on. Let's go."

"It's nothing to be embarrassed about," she said, following me as I led them speedily out of the auditorium. "Don't run away! This is your big moment! You were brilliant! Wasn't he brilliant?"

I didn't turn around to see who she was addressing this to. It could have been anyone.

Just when we seemed to be on the brink of escaping, Francine, draped in her usual billowing swaths of actory getup, launched herself out of a huddle of chatting parents and into my path. I could see from the terrifying gleam in her eyes that she was zeroing in on me.

I tried to change course, but she diverted swiftly and blocked my exit.

"Sam," she said, freezing me to the spot by placing a hand on my cheek. "You have something!"

Spoken by anyone else, those three words would have sounded trivial, but Francine loaded them with the somber portentousness of a newscaster announcing a stock market meltdown. I was tempted to respond with something defensively flippant, along the lines of, "What? Like lice?" but she was giving me a stare that banished all thoughts of humor.

"I don't say that lightly," she added unnecessarily, since she never said anything lightly. "We must talk. About your future."

"Um . . ."

"And you should have a think about your name."

"My name?"

"*Sam*," she said with a sneer, "is no name for someone with your gravitas. It's no name for an actor."

"I . . ."

"Don't say anything now. Just be. Absorb what you've achieved, and make sure you maintain your focus tomorrow. Intensity is all," she said.

"Okay. Thanks. I should go."

"You have a gift. Nurture it. Think of yourself as carrying everywhere you go a brimful glass of the most exquisite wine, which you mustn't spill. That wine is your talent."

"Okay. Maybe."

"Take care of it."

"Yeah. I have to go."

"Go! Be free!"

I went. As fast as I could.

Back home, Mom summoned me to the kitchen for a cup of tea and told me she had something to say. She put on her deep and meaningful voice (which is roughly a quarter as deep and meaningful as Francine's, but then she's never had the training), and looked into my eyes. We stared at each other in awkward silence for a while, and then she said, "I'm sorry."

As Mom's something-to-say proclamations go, this was unusually painless and fantastically brief. Though, of course, this was just a feed line. I knew there'd be more to come.

"Sorry for what?" I asked obediently.

"I underestimated you."

"Oh. That's okay."

Was that it? Was I really getting off this lightly? Could I leave?

"I know you didn't want to go to that school, and I admit I did think it would be better suited to Ethan and Freya."

"I know. That's fine. It is."

"But it's wonderful how you've thrived there."

"I wouldn't say 'thrived.'"

"What I mean is, you've found your talent. This is going to change everything for you."

"What—you think this means I'm now going to fit right in? Like all the other wannabes and show-offs that place is filled with?"

"The whole point of the school is to help you find your talent, and to nurture it. And you've done that! All this time you've been unhappy and lonely because you felt you didn't belong, and now you do!"

"Who says I want to belong?"

"Doesn't everyone?"

"Not with those people. Okay, I've made a few friends, and it's been pretty cool doing the play, but that doesn't make me an actor. It doesn't make me want to be part of Jennifer's gang, and it doesn't make me *gifted*."

"Yes it does! You were brilliant."

"It's a school play! I was okay, but I'm not going to be an actor. I don't even want to be an actor."

"Nobody's saying you have to be an actor."

"But you are saying I have to be *special*. You are saying that's what matters. And I don't buy that. How can everyone be special? Why should everyone even *want* to be special?"

"I'm just saying you were good. Better than I thought you'd be. Why are you getting angry with me?"

"Because you still want me to be somebody I'm not. Okay—so I can act a bit. Fine. That's not who I *am*. I'm just Sam. I'm the same Sam today as I was yesterday. I'm the same Sam as I was when we lived in Stevenage. I'm maybe a bit less afraid, a bit less shy, but that doesn't mean I think the only way to be significant is to get up on a stage."

"Well, that's good. I think it's excellent that you're so grounded. You probably didn't get that from me."

I looked down at my hands and brushed a stray sprinkling of salt into a tiny pile on the table. I could hear the grains scratching against the wood and the sound of my own breath.

"I should probably learn to be more like you and your father," added Mom wistfully. "I have this urge to do something *amazing*, but maybe that's why I always end up disappointed."

This was such an uncharacteristic thing for her to say, at first I couldn't believe my ears. Then it occurred to me that we were talking together almost like two adults. Which felt strange and wrong, yet also oddly right. Though if we really had been two adults, I probably would have been able to think of a reply. As it was, I just stared at her mutely, with the letters *W*, *T*, and *F* pinging around my skull.

"I don't want you to think I'm pushing you to be who you're not," she said.

I contemplated telling her this is exactly what she'd been making me feel ever since we'd moved to London, but instead I shrugged.

She reached across the table and took my hand. For once, I let her.

"I'm sorry," she said, almost as if she'd heard my unspoken response. "I'm proud of you. Not just of what you did tonight, but of who you are. And how you've

stayed true to yourself, even when it's made things difficult for you. That's a great quality."

She squeezed my hand. I kept on letting her, though I
was now getting very close to the upper limits of my toler-
ance for maternal physical contact.

Thankfully, Ethan burst in, puncturing the awkward
atmosphere. "Come on," he said. "We're late."

"Where are you going?" I asked, pulling my hand away
from Mom's.

"I booked a late-night rehearsal room. Don't want the
neighbors complaining," she said.

"You're . . . he asked you to . . . ?"

"Yup! I'm the new drummer," she replied proudly. "The
pan-global percussion seemed a strange fit at first, but
we're making it work."

"Darius is back too," said Ethan. "He likes the new sound.
And he thinks Mom's funny."

"Funny!?" she snapped.

"Not funny ha ha," Ethan backtracked. "Funny weird.
Not you! The setup. Weird in a good way. He says it's an
angle."

"That's great!" I said, trying to imagine what it would
look like to see Mom performing with Ethan's band, and
utterly failing. "So I should tell Felipe you're on for the cast
party?"

"Def!" said Mom.

"Don't say 'def,' " said Ethan.

"Yeah," I added. "Don't ever say 'def.' "

"Can I say 'fab'?"

"No."

" 'Lit'?"

"No."

"What am I supposed to say? Is it true that 'sick' now means 'good'?"

"No. 'Sick' is finished. It's over," said Ethan.

"So what do I say?"

"Just say nothing. Concentrate on the drumming."

"If you're rude to me, I'm going to hug you in public," threatened Mom.

"If you hug me in public you're out of the band."

"Guys!" I said. "Go and practice. I'll tell Felipe I've got live music for the party."

"Sick!" said Mom.

"Stop it," said Ethan. "That's just totally wrong. Stop trying."

"You're so discouraging!"

"You're so nuts!"

And off they went, bickering happily.

A first in the history of kissing

As Mr. Duverne had warned, the second performance was slightly flat. Everyone was a little too confident, perhaps insufficiently nervous, and when we sensed that the alchemy of the first night was somehow absent, everyone pushed that little bit harder to try and get it back, which made it recede even further.

The performance wasn't bad—nothing specific went wrong—it just lacked that suspension-of-the-rest-of-the-world quality that had made the opening night so special.

Afterward, when everyone had changed out of costume but was still milling around the backstage area, delaying the journey home, I approached Felipe and told him I'd found an up-and-coming band who'd do the cast party. I didn't say my brother was the guitarist, and certainly didn't mention my mom, but told him it was a group that had been put together by Darius (who everyone knew had a pop-star dad) and that they had just done a debut showcase (which was almost true).

He looked skeptical, but Jennifer, who was standing beside him with one hand in a back pocket of his jeans, leaped into the air, did her I'm-so-pleased-I'm-going-to-clap-like-a-trained-seal thing, and said, "Yay! Coool!"

"Are they any good?" said Felipe.

"Amazing," I lied, though this wasn't technically a complete lie because amazing doesn't necessarily mean "good." It can also mean "surprising" or "shocking" or even "hard to believe." I hadn't actually heard the band with the new middle-aged-mom-on-drums setup, but I felt pretty confident it would fit at least one of those descriptions.

"But everyone wants a DJ," said Felipe, though it was pretty clear the "everyone" he was referring to was just him.

"You could do it after," I said. "Like, you know, the headline act."

"And before," added Jennifer.

"And during," I said, which made Felipe's eyes glaze over with what I'd learned was his sarcasm-does-not-compute face.

"Okay. I guess," he replied, after giving up on his attempt to understand what I'd just said. "If that's what people want. I mean, I've got professional decks. And actual vinyl. Genuine."

He paused for a moment, waiting for Jennifer and me to give some kind of response to the vinyl brag, but neither of us managed to come up with anything.

"And proper DJ headphones," he added. "The whole kit."

"Wow," said Jennifer.

"Great," I said. "I'll tell the band."

For the third and final show, Mr. Duverne gave a pep talk to end all pep talks. There were tears, there was fist-pumping, motivational clapping was involved, and we were reminded several times that we would remember this for the rest of our lives. He told us he knew of "seasoned professionals—Tony-nominated stars—who still talk in dewy-eyed terms about their first student play."

As I crouched under the trapdoor during the first scene, waiting for my cue, I sensed in my blood that for this performance I was just the right amount of nervous. Not terrified, but not relaxed; tense but not edgy; absolutely ready with every fiber of my being to go up onstage, get called a dickhead in Shakespearean verse, and prance around dressed as a monster spitting curses at teenagers with glued-on beards. This wasn't going to be my life—it wasn't going to define me—but it sure was fun.

When the curtain went down after our final bows, muffling the stamping, whistling, and applause rising up from the crammed auditorium, a deluge of kissing, weeping, screaming, mutual backslapping, and more weeping overtook us. I ended up right in the middle of a lengthy group hug that involved the whole cast, and at one point I found myself squeezed in Jennifer's arms, with her saying in my ear, "We did it! We did it!"

Someone began to sing a song from the play, and even though it was a solo onstage, we'd all heard it so often that everyone knew the words and all of us joined in, until somehow, "*Full fathom five thy father lies / Of his bones are coral made / Those are pearls that were his eyes*" morphed into a rendition of "We Are the Champions."

As I took off my makeup, people kept grabbing me and telling me how good I'd been, often followed by long descriptions of how crap I was at first.

Instead of being involved in all the singing and messing around, Marina was busy gathering up everyone's costumes, darting from place to place with armfuls of coat hangers, robes, jackets, and dresses. When I handed her my leotard and mask, she opened her mouth, seemingly to say what everyone else had been saying, then closed it again, smiled and placed the palm of her hand on my chest. For a moment, I felt as if we were enclosed in a bubble of intimate silence, shielded from the din around us.

"I always knew you'd be great," she said eventually.

"It would have been a disaster without that mask. You saved my life."

She shook her head. "You did it yourself."

"I really didn't."

Felipe then appeared, announced that he didn't know where to put his costume, and dumped a heap of sweaty clothes into Marina's arms. His Prince of the Kingdom of Wedgie pants slithered to the floor, and by the time I'd picked them up, Marina was already being dragged away to resolve an emergency involving someone who was stuck in a corset. I called after her that I'd see her at the party, but she didn't seem to hear me.

When Mr. Duverne appeared backstage, the entire cast was half-naked, singing "Let It Go" at the top of our voices. Even me. If you'd told me one month ago that I'd soon find myself arm in arm with a gang of classmates, wearing only a pair of underpants and smears of green makeup, happily belting out Disney hits, I would not have believed you. In fact, I would have been entirely sure you were making fun of me. But as it turns out, you just never know what's ahead of you.

Mr. Duverne got a huge cheer, which eventually subsided as he stood on a chair and gave one last weepy speech. After Ulf handed over a cast present, which consisted of a huge box of chocolates and a hankie embroidered with the phrase "WRING AFTER USE," the girls retreated to their changing room to begin the lengthy process of getting dressed up for the party, and the atmosphere gradually calmed down to one of mere exultant hysteria.

Eventually, a motorcade left the school parking lot, with each vehicle containing at least six singing, shouting, or screaming teenagers and one parent at the wheel wearing a dazed but stoical how-did-my-life-come-to-this expression.

I ended up in the trunk of a Saab station wagon, sharing a dog bed with Ulf, who I could tell had succumbed to the mood of crazed elation because there was a slight smile playing at the corners of his mouth.

Nobody was in any doubt that Felipe's party was going to be epic. An enormous hormone stew had been bubbling away for weeks now, through the entire rehearsal period, and tonight it would come to a boil. Everyone knew it. These were the last few hours we would spend together as a group, and everything that had been held back would now, with the aid of a supply of illicitly procured alcohol, be unleashed. This, after all, is what parties are for. Or so I'd heard.

Within seconds of Felipe firing up his decks, the sexual tension became so intense it was like standing in a sauna of lust. As the house filled with guests, and the guests filled with alcohol, the pitch of randiness cranked ever higher.

I helped myself to a drink and hovered by the door, waiting for Marina to arrive. After a while I did a circuit of the whole party, looking for her, but she was nowhere to be found. When I asked Jennifer (who was in the middle of the living room, doing something that looked like a cross between flamenco dancing and twerking to a dubstep soundtrack) if she'd seen Marina anywhere, her response was, "Who?"

This was when I realized that only the actors and their friends had arrived. I'd assumed everyone involved in the play would be coming, but none of the lighting, set, props, or costume people had appeared.

I had finally made it to a proper party. I had finally made a genuine connection with a girl. Everything seemed to be coming together, but now, at the key moment, it had all fallen apart again. Even here, surrounded by what looked like an exceptionally enthusiastic mouth-to-mouth resuscitation practice session, I had found a way to be alone.

I went over to Felipe, who was at his decks with a

massive pair of headphones cupped over one ear, and asked what had happened.

"The techies?" he said. "Oh God, I didn't invite them. What a bunch of geeks!"

"We're a team. You can't have a cast party and leave them out! We couldn't have done any of it without them."

"Well, they'll just have to put on their own party. There's a limit to numbers. Honestly, I had to leave out practically half of my actual friends."

"You invited other people, but not the techies who made the play possible?"

"Only cool people."

"But—"

"Listen—when's the band coming?"

"You can't—'

"Just tell me when the band's coming. My set has to build to a climax. I can't just stop in mid-flow. I'm a DJ, not a tap."

"This is supposed to be the cast party," I said.

"What time? I need to know," he said, ignoring my protests.

"Soon. I'll check."

I turned, pushed through the thicket of sweaty bodies, and messaged Ethan, who said he was on his way, then Marina.

Where are you? I've been looking everywhere for you.

At the party. The geek party. You at Felipe's?

Yes! Come!

Not invited.

I'm inviting you now!

Too late. Apparently I'm not good enough.

Felipe's a dick! I had no idea you weren't invited.

Why are you at his house if you think he's a dick?

Because it's a party. And my brother's band's playing. What's your party like?

Shit. Everyone's standing around moaning about how smug actors are.

So come here.

To be with the smug actors?

I'm not smug.

He said smugly.

I'm not. Come! Please! xx

Maybe. I might just go home. I'm feeling kind of pissed off.

Do you have any idea how much I wish you were here?

I'm not invited.

That doesn't matter.

It does to me.

I sent her the address just as Ethan arrived with his guitar, his bandmates, and our mother.

When she entered the party, Mom froze in the doorway and stared. The room was now crammed with couples doing the kind of slow dancing that involved no movement of the legs; heavy use of hands, groin, and lips; and had far more to do with procreation than dance. The only person looking remotely animated was Felipe, who was standing behind his decks with a laser pointer in each hand, gesticulating wildly to his Ibiza Euro-house upbeat party hits as if to a megaclub of amped-up ravers rather than to a chintzy living room filled with oblivious kids entirely absorbed in exploring the early stages of foreplay. He could have been playing the theme song to *PAW Patrol* and it would have made no difference whatsoever.

I watched Mom taking in the distinctly R-rated vibe, and for a moment I was worried she might switch on the lights and launch into a family-planning lecture. I saw the thought cross her mind, but instead of acting on it, she put on an I-haven't-seen-what-I-just-saw expression and made her way to the stage area in the corner.

The band took a while to set up, particularly Darius, who was using enough cable to rewire a telephone switchboard. While his mission-control-style electronics hub took shape, and Mom practiced the tambourine, Cass and Ethan retreated to a dark corner and began to make out.

I'd been wondering why Ethan had been in such a cheerful mood the past couple of days. This explained it.

When they were eventually ready, the band started so loudly that even the dancers in an advanced state of physical arousal pried themselves apart and began to respond to the music. Soon everyone was leaping up and down in place, and I sensed a ripple of amusement travel through the room as people noticed who was playing the drums.

Mom hadn't been to a gig since the 1980s, and appeared to have forgotten, in the course of getting dressed up, that the intervening thirty years had taken place. She'd done something to her hair that made it stand on end, and was wearing a leopard-print top with acid-washed jeans that must have been hiding at the back of a wardrobe since long before I was even born. Her face was plastered in enough makeup to paint a battleship.

This could quite easily have been the most embarrassing moment of my life, but she was so lost in her drumming—so absolutely committed to her performance—that the question of embarrassment was somehow blown away. In fact, even though she looked utterly ridiculous, I had never seen her do anything remotely so cool. I remembered her amazement, after my first performance, that I wasn't in fact a useless actor, and realized that I was now thinking the exact same thing about her drumming. It had simply never occurred to me that she might be good.

Cass was at the other end of the fashion-embarrassment scale, wearing a PVC catsuit that left very little to the imagination and rendered me faintly light-headed. The idea that she was my geeky, pasty-faced brother's girlfriend was almost impossible to believe. It really is astonishing what an electric guitar can do for a guy.

My if-you-don't-care-about-embarrassment-you-can't-be-embarrassed theory was pushed to the very limit by Mom's drum solo, which, judging by the look on Ethan's face, went on considerably longer than had been rehearsed. An interlude on tambourine and bongo drums, containing elements of interpretive dance, was particularly high-risk, but she got away with it by surfing an audience response of sheer disbelief.

By the end, rivers of sweat were pouring down the insides of the windows, and the room smelled like the hippo enclosure at London Zoo. The band did three encores, even though they didn't know any more songs.

When they finally switched off and unplugged, the party fell silent. Or seemed to. I couldn't actually tell, because my ears were now ringing at the volume of a burglar alarm.

I fought my way toward the stage to congratulate Mom and Ethan. They both gabbled enthusiastically at me but I couldn't hear a word they were saying, so I just gave them each a hug and shouted in their ears that I was proud of them. For some reason this made Mom cry, which was kind of embarrassing, so I made an exit and told them we'd talk later.

I did yet another search of the house to see if Marina had arrived, but there was no sign of her. Then I spotted Jennifer at the edge of the dance floor, staring across the living room with a livid expression on her face, seemingly on the brink of an explosion of tears or violence or both.

I followed her eyeline and saw Felipe, on the sofa, entwined with a long-haired, long-legged, hot-pants-wearing girl who had arrived as part of his gang of "cool people." Either he had lost an important peanut inside her bra or they were sharing an intimate moment in a not very private place.

I looked back toward Jennifer and found her standing right in front of me, wearing an expression of psychotic fury.

"Look at him!" she said, her voice an octave or two higher than usual.

"I've seen."

"What a scumbag! What an absolute asshole! Can you believe it!?"

"Yes" was the answer that immediately sprang to mind, but it seemed more tactful to just shrug and say nothing.

"After everything I did for him! Forgiving him! Taking him back!"

"That's the kind of guy he is," I said.

"Do you think I'm going to let him treat me like that? *Do you?*" she yelled, her eyes narrowing to vengeful slits.

"Don't get angry with me."

"I'm not angry with you."

"You sound angry."

"Of course I'm angry! Nobody . . . *nobody* . . . treats Jennifer Salisbury like that. Not now. Not ever."

"Did you just talk about yourself in the third person? That's kind of weird."

"Two can play at that game, you know."

"What game?"

Jennifer took my hand in a steely grip and pulled me across the room. When we were in front of Felipe, she grabbed me by the head, yanked me toward her face, and kissed me. Hard. Like she was trying to suck out my teeth.

After all the hours I'd spent dreaming about exactly this, I was surprised to discover that the reality had nothing whatsoever in common with my fantasies, but in fact reminded me of a visit to the dentist.

Jennifer paused her face-vacuuming kiss and looked across at Felipe to see if he'd noticed. He hadn't. The search was still on for that missing peanut.

I took a step back, struggling to think of a way to explain that I didn't want to get involved in her argument with Felipe, but before I could say anything or withdraw any further, she gripped my T-shirt, pulled me toward her, and resumed the procedure with even greater force.

Never before in the history of kissing can there have been such a gulf between anticipation and reality. There was a time when just imagining this taking place would have diverted my entire blood supply southward; now it was actually happening, for real, and I had the feeling that my dick, by some biological miracle, was shrinking.

Just as viscerally as I had once wanted to get close to Jennifer, I now wanted to get away from her. But however bad a situation may be, it's worth remembering that things can always get worse. When she finally paused and her grip slackened, I turned aside to catch a breath and my eyes immediately fell on the living room doorway, where Marina was standing, staring right at me. The look in her eyes was one of pure loathing.

I twisted free of Jennifer and hurried toward Marina, fighting my way through the slimy whirl of partygoers, but it was too late. She had spun on her heels and fled. By the time I got out onto the street, she was gone.

I ran around the block searching for her, but she'd vanished.

I WhatsApped her; I texted her; I even phoned her. Nothing.

I ran around two more blocks in the other direction.

No sign.

Eventually, lost in a backstreet I didn't recognize, I sat on a curb, feet in the gutter, and buried my head in my hands.

The lyrics of Ethan's attempt at solo songwriting began to pound around my head. His words, which on first hearing had appeared hollow and self-indulgent, now seemed to get to the very essence of life. He'd hit on a powerful eternal truth. Everything *was* shit. That was the human condition, in a nutshell, right there.

Marina had come to the party to find me. If I hadn't behaved like an utter moron, if I'd had it in me to stand up to Jennifer, at this very moment I'd be tangling tongues with the girl I liked more than anyone else I had ever met. Instead, I was sitting in a gutter with my head in my hands, lost, humming "Shitty shitty shit shit."

My brother had the musical talent, the beautiful girl-friend, and maybe even the makings of a poet. I had nothing.

... and we didn't even slightly care

Ethan's good fortune, however, didn't last.

The first indication that something had gone wrong was when he spent twenty-four hours facedown on the living room sofa, groaning. This happened only a day after his seemingly triumphant gig at the cast party.

Everyone knows rock stars have short careers, but even for a musician this seemed like a fast burnout. When Mom asked him what had happened, he just said, "I'M FINE," which wasn't very convincing. If anyone else asked, he either grunted or said, "Leave me alone," which was at least a bit more honest.

The following evening, despite his protests that he wasn't hungry and couldn't eat, Mom broke her all-meals-at-the-table rule and left him a tray of food. When I was sent to the living room half an hour later to collect the plate, it had been picked clean and Ethan seemed marginally cheered up, by which I mean he was still facedown on the sofa but had stopped groaning.

I asked how he was feeling, and he said, "Maybe I should just cut my dick off and give it to charity."

This seemed like a pretty good indication that his woes were of a romantic nature.

"I don't think Goodwill accepts severed genitals," I said, which is the kind of lighthearted banter Ethan normally enjoys, but there was no response.

When a joke backfires you have two choices. You can either back off or push on. It's pretty much always better to take the first option, but that's something I never seem to remember when it matters.

"To have any resale value they really have to be in mint condition," I said, "and frankly . . ."

Ethan raised himself from the horizontal and gave me an unamused stare. Patchy tufts of stubble were sprouting from his sallow, milk-white face; his eyes were puffy and bloodshot; his chin was glistening with half-dried drool; and his breath smelled like a drain. "Why would she dump me?" he asked plaintively.

A number of answers immediately occurred to me, but I kept them to myself.

"I mean, one minute everything's amazing and loved-up

and fantastic," he continued, "and the next she's just turned on me. Goodbye. Over."

"Did she give a reason?"

"Not really."

"Did you ask?"

"Yes! And she just fobbed me off with all the usual 'It's not you, it's me' stuff, then it turns out she's gotten back together with Veronika and the band has re-formed without me."

"Oh. Right. So you're kind of dumped as a boyfriend and a guitarist."

"Yeah, thanks for spelling that out. I appreciate that."

"Sorry."

"So when I heard that, I just kept calling her and telling her it wasn't fair and she had to give me a reason, and she kept saying I should leave her alone and that she didn't have to explain herself if she didn't want to, then eventually she said she'd never really tried having a boyfriend before and it was interesting but she'd realized it wasn't her thing."

"Interesting?"

"Yeah. Interesting. So I told her I didn't understand what she was talking about, and she said I was too penile."

"Too penile?"

"Will you stop repeating all the most depressing words I say?"

"Sorry . . . I just . . . what does that even mean?"

"I don't know! I'm a guy! I'm penile! What did she expect?"

"How penile were you?"

"A normal amount! I was averagely penile!"

"For a guy."

"Exactly."

"A guy who's straight but is pretending to be bisexual in the hope that it'll make his band more interesting."

Ethan's mouth froze into a thoughtful pout. "What are you saying?"

"Just . . . you know . . . maybe this isn't about her turning on you. It might be about you pretending to be what you're not and getting found out. Maybe if you're straight you should tell people you're straight, and look for a girlfriend who . . . you know . . . wants a boyfriend."

Ethan stared at the floor. For a second or two he seemed to stop breathing, then he looked up, blinked, and said, "What are you? The Dalai Lama?"

"I'm just saying maybe you're not the victim here."

"Okay," he said, "what's going to happen now is I'm going to punch you."

"Why? I haven't done anything."

"It's for your own good."

He punched me, quite hard, on the arm. I took this as a sign of his mood taking a turn for the better.

"Why'd you do that?"

"To stop you from getting smug."

"You do realize," I said, "that was an extremely penile act."

"ALL RIGHT! You're dead!"

He leaped at me but I was too quick. I sprinted out of the room and down the stairs with Ethan close behind. He caught up with me in the kitchen, where he tackled me to the ground, sat on my chest, and attempted to suffocate me with a stuffed unicorn.

Out of the corner of my eye I spotted Mom beaming from ear to ear, radiating relief at the restoration of family harmony.

"Get off!" I said eventually, spitting out tufts of pink unicorn hide. "I'm still hungry."

"Me too," said Ethan. "Absolutely starving."

Dad passed him an empty plate, which he loaded with a compost-heap-size portion of pasta.

Between mouthfuls, Ethan mumbled, "By the way, I've decided I'm straight."

"Okay," said Mom. "As long as you're happy."

I really never expected her to take it so well.

"Other big news is that you and me have been chucked out of the band," he added.

"Both of us?"

"Yes."

"Is that why you're so upset?"

"Partly. It's a long story."

"A long and penile story," I said.

"What?" asked Mom.

"Painful. A long and painful story."

Ethan kicked me under the table. I kicked him back.

"So will you start a new band?" asked Dad.

"I dunno. Maybe. What about you, Mom?"

"Me?"

"Your drumming was pretty good. Maybe *you* should look for a new band."

"Oh no," said Mom. "That's over. Finished. I've had my fun."

"No more drumming?"

"I'm going to put them in the attic."

"Why?" asked Dad.

"I have no use for them at the moment. I don't think I need the workshop anymore either, actually. If you want it as a garden shed, I'll clear it out."

Mom was using a casual voice, but everyone noticed this was a major declaration.

"How come?" said Dad.

"I just feel like I've gotten something out of my system. I think maybe this whole journey I've taken has been a kind of sabbatical."

"A . . .?"

"Like a vacation," said Mom, preempting Freya's inevitable question. "When we lived in Stevenage, I always thought I was only working to earn money, so when we stopped needing the money I was thrilled to walk out. But I think maybe I need it. As a focus for my energies."

"You do have quite a lot of energies," said Dad tentatively.

"I need a bit more rigor in my life."

"Rigor is when your body goes stiff after someone's killed you by touching your pressure points, isn't it?" said Freya. "Hannah's big brother told me."

"That's rigor mortis, sweetie, which is a different thing. Rigor is another word for discipline. It's when you do things because they feel important, so you have to do them, instead of just trying to have fun all the time. And I'm not sure you should have any more playdates at Hannah's house. Maybe you could invite her here instead."

"Why?" asked Freya.

"I'm going to retrain," said Mom, ignoring Freya's question and turning to face Dad. "As a music therapist. I want to help people who haven't had our good luck. I think it'll be fulfilling."

A note of confidence and finality in her voice made it clear this wasn't a hazy notion, a vague plan, or another passing fad. This was a serious decision, and she was going to see it through.

Mom and Dad locked eyes, and the rest of us stared at them staring at each other. I could feel Freya itching to ask what a music therapist was, but she somehow sensed this was a significant adult moment and kept quiet.

"Sounds like a great idea," said Dad, reaching out and taking Mom's hand.

"Yeah—I think you'll be good at it," I said.

"You do?" said Mom, her voice ringing with surprise.

"You'll be awesome. You're a natural," said Ethan.

Mom laughed, which was strange, since no one had said anything funny, then a second later it looked as if she might be about to cry.

"What's a music therapist?" said Freya. She has her limits.

"If you don't mind, I really would love that shed," said Dad. "I'm beginning to think sheds might suit me better than offices. I've had a new idea I want to start tinkering with."

"It's yours," said Mom. "Have it."

"Great."

"The course I've found is full-time," said Mom, patting Dad's hand, "so maybe you could help out and do a bit more of the cooking."

"NO!" yelled Ethan and Freya and me simultaneously.

"NOT DAD'S COOKING!" said Freya.

"Please!" I said.

"We'll all starve! Or be poisoned!" said Ethan.

"Sure," said Dad. "No problem."

The two of them gazed at each other across the table again, with big, stupid smiles on their faces, and after a while a strange twinkle began to appear in their eyes.

I almost can't describe what happened next because it is frankly so disgusting. Mom and Dad got up, left the room, and went upstairs. Together.

Okay, before I actually puke, I'm going to move on to the important thing here, which is the catastrophic implosion of my nonexistent love life. You wouldn't have thought that something which didn't even exist could go wrong, or that something which had always been a failure could find new ways to fail, but I was learning that both these things were possible.

The first school day after the party, Jennifer greeted me with the timeworn phrase "Great party. I was sooo drunk," which, despite my total inexperience of parties, getting drunk, kissing the wrong person, or indeed kissing anyone at all, even I recognized as code for, "Let's pretend that what happened didn't happen."

"Yeah," I replied emphatically. "Great party. I was sooo drunk too."

She seemed hugely relieved by this response. The fact that both of us had been drinking Coke was cut-and-pasted from history.

Marina, however, wouldn't talk to me. For days, I sent her messages every hour, saying that I needed to talk to her, that the thing she had seen didn't mean what it looked like, that Jennifer had just grabbed me and I was trying to get away from her, but Marina never answered. My explanation clearly didn't sound plausible, and I could see why. In her position, I wouldn't have believed me either. In fact, I'd be convinced that I was a lying sleazeball.

I needed to speak to her. There was no way to convincingly explain myself in a message, but whenever I got near her at school she turned and walked away. In classes, she always positioned herself as far away from me as possible, and however hard I tried, I could never get her to make eye contact. It was as if she had simply erased me. Made me invisible to her.

I was used to feeling invisible, of course, but never like this, never in a way that felt like a personal slap across the face.

The strange thing was that in the wake of the play, with everyone other than Marina I was suddenly, for the first time, popular. And visible. People who had never before given me a second glance were now friendly. Even Psycho Steve greeted me with a nod when we passed each other in a corridor. Everyone in the school seemed to have shifted their attitude toward me from indifference to acceptance. Marina, meanwhile, had traveled the same path but in the opposite direction, in fact traveling beyond indifference all the way to outright hostility.

This felt like a brutal injustice, though I knew I had only myself to blame.

After more than a week of this, I was beginning to think I'd have to give up on Marina forever (and possibly on girls in general and any hope of successfully losing my virginity before the onset of baldness, halitosis, and impotence). Then, on the way home from school, I spotted someone at a bus stop wearing an outfit made from a menagerie of soft toy animals flattened out and sewed together to make a kind of surreal parody of a fur coat. I realized immediately this could only be Marina. As I was contemplating approaching her, a bus pulled over and she got on.

Optimistic brain and pessimistic brain both froze, but brain number three must have stepped into the power vacuum, because next thing I knew I was running for the bus and squeezing myself on board just as the doors closed.

Marina saw me, frowned, and turned to look out the window. I approached her seat slowly, arriving at the same moment that the bus lurched around a corner, which almost sent me flying into her lap headfirst. Luckily, I stopped this from happening by crashing my skull against a metal bar.

"Ow! Shit!" I said, which wasn't the greeting I'd been preparing.

I saw her almost ask if I was okay, then stop herself.

"Is this seat free?" I asked, rubbing the bump on my forehead.

She ignored me.

I sat next to her.

"Are you following me?" she said.

"No."

"You live down that way, don't you?"

"Yeah."

"So where are you going?"

"This way."

"Why?"

"A visit. To a person. Okay—look, I'm not following you but I saw you get on this bus and I just jumped on without thinking. I have to talk to you. I need to explain. This is killing me."

"You don't look very dead. Unfortunately."

"Listen—what I said in my messages is true. I know it's hard to believe, but it is. Felipe was on the sofa with this girl—I don't even know who she was—but it wasn't Jennifer, and Jennifer was staring at them with this *I'm going to kill him* face on, then she saw me and steered me over right in front of him and started to kiss me. She just grabbed me. Honestly. And I admit, I did like her once, and there was a time when I would have really wanted that to happen, but since I've gotten to know you that changed completely and the whole thing with Jennifer was over in a second, and it was actually just weird and unpleasant. I didn't want her to do it and I didn't enjoy it. I've got no interest in her. I like you."

Marina was no longer looking out of the window, but she wasn't turned toward me either. I examined her profile closely, watching her eyes assess me at a sharp, skeptical angle.

"A second?" she said.

"Maybe five seconds. Max."

"You didn't instigate it?"

"No! I didn't even want her to do it!"

"Really?"

"Yes!"

"And you didn't enjoy it?"

"No! I don't like her. She's selfish and fake and annoying."

"But you're a guy. That doesn't mean you don't like her. Everyone likes her."

"Okay—there was a period when I liked her and thought she was cute, then a phase when I didn't like her but still thought she was cute, then I ended up disliking her so much that I stopped thinking she was even slightly cute and couldn't even remember why I thought it in the first place."

"Are you really trying to tell me Jennifer was all over you, and you were standing there wanting her to stop?"

"Yes! I swear!"

"It didn't look that way."

"What are you talking about? I was fighting for breath! My dick actually shrank."

"You didn't need to tell me that."

"It did!"

"Really. That's not information I need to know."

"Hand on heart, it shrank. It shriveled."

"Stop!"

"Not to nothing. I'm just saying it got smaller."

"Enough!"

"So about that movie," I said.

"Which movie?"

"The one we were thinking of going to see."

"We never chose one."

"Would you like to?"

"Maybe."

"How about this Saturday?"

"Maybe."

"Is that a yes-maybe or a no-maybe?"

"I'll think about it."

"It's a yes-maybe, isn't it?"

"Probably."

"Probably! I'm getting somewhere now."

"Listen—don't mess me around and don't be a prick! Because I'm not up for that."

"This is so romantic."

"You're actually miles from home now. You realize that, don't you?"

"I can't get off until I've moved you on from probably."

"Okay, yes. I'll go."

"YESSSSSSSSSSSSSSSSSSSSS! YES!"

"Don't be cocky. And I still think you behaved like an asshole at that party."

"I know. I'm sorry."

"What are you doing?"

"Nothing."

"You're leaning in."

"Am I?"

"Just because I've said yes to a date, that doesn't mean

you can just lean into my space and look like you want to kiss me."

"Doesn't it? I can't help how I look."

"We're on a bus."

"I know."

"In public."

"Yeah, but you talking about me looking as if I want to kiss you has made me want to kiss you even more."

"Well, find something else to think about."

"I can't. You're thinking about it too, aren't you?"

"Maybe a bit."

I gave her a long, steady look, examining her clear green eyes, her long eyelashes, her soft lips. She looked back at me, holding my gaze.

"What are you thinking about now?" I asked.

"Same thing," she said. "It's getting worse."

"Well, maybe if we're both thinking it, perhaps we should just, kind of . . ."

I never got to finish my sentence.

Marina missed her stop, and the bus driver had to kick us out at the terminus. Neither of us had any idea where we were, and we didn't even slightly care.

Acknowledgments

Thank you Hannah Sandford, Felicity Rubinstein, Rebecca McNally, Lizz Skelly, Cat Anderson at the Edinburgh Bookshop, and, above all, for all the usual innumerable reasons plus the extra one of telling me to write this book, Maggie O'Farrell.